1 MONTH OF
FREE
READING

at

www.ForgottenBooks.com

By purchasing this book you are
eligible for one month membership to
ForgottenBooks.com, giving you
unlimited access to our entire
collection of over 1,000,000 titles via
our web site and mobile apps.

To claim your free month visit:

www.forgottenbooks.com/free233069

ISBN 978-0-483-12283-3
PIBN 10233069

HIS GRACE

BY

W. E. NORRIS

AUTHOR OF "MDLE. DE MERSAC," "THE ROGUE,"
"MARCIA," "JAUK'S FATHER," ETC.

IN TWO VOLUMES

VOL. II.

Methuen & Co.
18 BURY STREET, LONDON, W.C.
1892

CONTENTS

——o——

CHAPTER I.

CHAPTER IX.

CHAPTER X.

CHAPTER XI.

HIS GRACE

HIS GRACE.

—o—

CHAPTER I.

A MYSTERIOUS MENACE.

WE all went early to bed; for, although Mr Gascoigne's cigars were excellent, his personal attractions were scarcely strong enough to detain two weary men in the smoking-room for more than half-an-hour, and Hurstbourne was too sleepy to go on sparring with him. As for me, I was tired rather than heavy-headed, sleep having been murdered, in my case, by the distressing reflections with which that old woman had provided me, and which indeed kept me tossing to and fro half the night through.

It does not seem probable that Miss St George's slumbers were seriously interfered with by any outspoken remonstrances which may have reached her from the same quarter; though it is likely enough that she was remonstrated with before her aunt wished her good-night, and when the next morning reunited our congenial party at the breakfast-table, I thought I could perceive in the young lady's face and manner symptoms of something of the kind having taken place. But, perhaps, like many better persons than herself, she was apt to be a little silent and sulky at breakfast time.

Possibly she may have been neither the one nor the other when we had finished our meal and when she managed to give her chaperon the slip. At least, when I say that she gave her chaperon the slip, I only mean that she did a thing which her chaperon had not courage or presence of mind enough to forbid, not that she stooped to any subterfuge. She announced, without the slightest hesitation, that she was going round to the stables with the Duke, who wanted to have a look at his horses; and, as Mr Gascoigne presently saw fit to follow the couple, it fell to my lot to receive a second homily from Lady Deverell, with which, since it was in all essentials identical with that already reported, I need not weary the reader. I myself was not a little wearied by it, and was more than a little rejoiced when at length Hurstbourne re-appeared to give me my marching orders.

"We may as well ride home, Martyn," said he. "The grey is all right again, and I'll send for our traps in the course of the afternoon. All things considered, we may congratulate ourselves upon not having paid too long a price for a real good day's sport."

"That is most flattering to us," remarked Miss St George, who had accompanied him into the room. "Tedious as you have naturally found us, you feel that a good run has compensated you for the nuisance of having had to submit to us for one evening. Luckily, we sha'n't have the chance of putting your forbearance to the test a second time."

"I only wish there were a chance of your testing it every evening for the next six months!" responded Hurstbourne with fervour.

Whereupon Miss St George laughed, and ob-

served that the forbearance of other people
might be tried rather too highly if that polite
aspiration could be fulfilled.

The forbearance of Mr Gascoigne had, I
think, been already strained about as far as
it would go. He did not accompany us to the
door. He merely shook hands with us, and
said rather coldly that he hoped we would do
him the favour to make use of his stables, at
any future time that might be convenient to
us. He was afraid that he should not be able
to offer us house-room again, because his Par-
liamentary duties would compel him to go up
to London shortly.

Lady Deverell gave Hurstbourne the tips of
her fingers, and was kind enough to place the
whole five of them within my grasp, saying—

"Good-bye. My love to your sister. You
had better tell her what I have told you.
If she won't listen, so much the worse for
her."

Miss St George did not appear to see me
until I was upon the point of vanishing from
her view, when she honoured me with a vague

bow; but she whispered something, which I did not catch, to Hurstbourne, on taking leave of him.

"What did that old pussy-cat mean?" inquired the latter, after we had mounted our horses and were riding down the avenue. "What was it that she told you?"

"Nothing of any consequence," I replied. "As far as I can recollect, it didn't amount to much more than that I was a bad lot, and that you were another, and that Nora ought not be living with people of our shady character."

I thought that would stimulate his curiosity, and provoke him to put further queries, which I should not have been reluctant to answer, with a due regard to discretion; but it did not produce that effect upon him. He only laughed and said—

"Oh! that was all, eh?"

We had advanced some little distance on our way, without exchanging another word, when he turned upon me with a sudden and unexpected question:

"I say, Martyn, did you ever hear what was the cause of my old uncle's quarrel with my father?"

I shook my head.

"I never heard anything about it. I never was in the way of hearing. Was there any cause, except incompatibility of temper?"

"That's just what I don't know, and what I have often wondered. I can't ask my mother, because she gets distressed, and begins to cry, and all that, you know, if the subject is introduced. I thought perhaps Lady Deverell might have told you something. Whatever it was, I suspect that beggar Paul knows a good deal about it."

He added, with a short laugh, after pausing for a minute or two—

"Well, I've put our cool friend Paul's back up, anyhow. Do you know that, when we were up at the stables just now, he dragged me off, upon the pretence of showing me a couple of colts, to ask me in plain language what my intentions were with regard to Miss St George?"

"Oh, he did, did he?" said I. "And what answer did you make?"

"The only answer that could be made. I said I would thank him to mind his own business. Then he had the cheek to tell me that I should consult my own interests best by keeping friends with him, that he felt more or less responsible for Miss St George while she was his guest and that, if I chose to defy him, he might be compelled to make things uncomfortable for me. Naturally, I defied him then and there, after which he began hinting that there was some disgraceful mystery connected with my father which he could disclose if he were driven to it. It is true that he retracted when I — well, when I pointed out to him what would happen unless he either spoke out or apologised; but I don't think I really misunderstood him, though he assured me that I had."

Now, I certainly had heard that the late Lord Charles Gascoigne had been an old rip, and it seemed quite on the cards that he might have done something disgraceful in the

days of his youth; but there was no particular
use in saying that. I therefore only said
what I believed to be true, that our late host
was not precisely a hero and that he was
evidently jealous. People who are suffering
from the pangs of jealousy and who are not
dowered with a chivalrous nature frequently,
I observed, threaten more than they can perform. Mr Gascoigne's empty words were of
no importance, except in so far as they served
to throw some additional light upon his in-
dividuality.

Hurstbourne accepted this explanation; it is
his way to accept any explanation which
relieves his honest mind of harassing mis-
givings. He shook his shoulders, and chuckled,
and said—

"The idea of that chicken - hearted fellow
flattering himself that a girl of Miss St
George's pluck would look twice at him! He
does lay that flattering unction to his soul,
though."

"Why," I asked, "shouldn't a plucky girl
marry a chicken-hearted man? Always sup-

posing that he is rich enough. I can't imagine a more courageous act, and, saving your presence, I shouldn't be a bit surprised if Miss St George were to prove herself capable of it."

"That's what we shall see if we live long enough," returned Hurstbourne, gathering up his reins. "Now, I don't believe it would do these horses any harm to have a gentle canter across the grass."

CHAPTER II.

AN ASSIGNATION.

WE did not, on our return home, meet with quite the warmest of welcomes; and I suppose Hurstbourne's conscience and prescience must have alike disquieted him, for, as we drew near the huge edifice of which he was sole lord and master, he began to assume something of the air of a schoolboy who has broken out of bounds.

"I expect my mother won't be over and above pleased at our having spent the night at Lavenham," he remarked, in a confidential tone, while we were dismounting; "she'll be sure to say that we had no business to accept hospitality from Paul. But we really couldn't help it, could we?"

"*I* couldn't help it," I replied, rather ungenerously; "I don't know so much about you."

"My dear fellow, neither you nor I could have ridden another half - mile without gross cruelty to animals. Besides, I thought we had all agreed that Paul was to be treated with friendliness. Goodness knows, it's no pleasure to me to eat the fellow's food or to drink his wine!"

The above feeble excuses were all that he had to offer to Lady Charles, who, as he had anticipated, took him to task with some severity for having sojourned in the tents of the ungodly.

"I can't see what was to prevent Paul Gascoigne from sending you home, considering that he was able to send a dog-cart to fetch your clothes," she pertinently remarked. "Why on earth did he want you to stay with him?"

"Oh, if you come to that, I don't know that he did so very particularly want it," replied that foolish Hurstbourne, thereby, of course, answering all the questions which his mother had not put.

Lady Charles grunted and looked wise. After-

wards she condescended to cross-examine me;
though I think that she did not stoop so far
without a preliminary struggle between her
pardonable curiosity and her sense of what was
due to the exalted station in which Providence
had placed her. I did not tell her a great deal
about Miss St George; because, as I was able
to assure her with perfect sincerity, I knew
very little about that supercilious young lady;
but whether I had spoken or whether I had
held my tongue, she would soon have known
as much as I did. We could not find Miss St
George in any of the social books of reference
to which we had recourse; but it stood to reason
that if she was Lady Deverell's niece, she must
be well-born, so that the chief question appeared
to be whether she was physically and mentally
fitted to carry on the illustrious line of the
Gascoignes. That, Lady Charles declared, was
really the sole point which concerned her;
Arthur must choose for himself, and she would
not dream of opposing his choice unless it
should be a manifestly unwise one. All the
same, I don't think she was free from maternal

jealousy, and I don't think she was displeased when I confessed that Miss St George had failed to secure my personal admiration.

"Of course," said she, with the air of worldly wisdom which she was fond of assuming, and which always seemed to me rather pathetic considering what a goose the poor woman really was—"of course the girl is trying to catch him. Unfortunately, that is what they all try to do, and there is no help for it. Still, it doesn't follow that she may not make as good a wife as another. I must manage to see her somehow and have a talk with her."

I suppose it was rather stupid of me to observe that, even if Miss St George should not succeed in espousing the head of the family, the honour of having brought future generations of Gascoignes into the world might still be hers; for I conscientiously believed the match to be an undesirable one, and I ought to have done what I could towards imbuing Lady Charles with my sentiments. But the moment that she realised the rivalry which existed between her son and her nephew she took a side; and, naturally, it was the wrong side. Without admitting this in so many words, she nevertheless made it plain to a not very acute bystander, and I perceived, to my regret, that Hurstbourne was not going to be scolded or thwarted any more.

As for me, I received a wholly unmerited scolding from Nora, who chose to take it for granted that I had talked her over with Lady Deverell, and who, when I could not deny that she and her actions had been made the subject of some discussion, said it was rather unfair to discuss her behind her back. She was slightly mollified on hearing that I had not divulged her intention of jilting Mr Burgess; but I did not deem the occasion an appropriate one for stating that, in my opinion, that intention ought not any longer to be kept secret. She did not mention Miss St George; nor did I. Alas! she was likely to hear all that she wanted to hear, and perhaps a little more, about Miss St George before she was much older.

I had work to do both in the afternoon and

evening, which was a blessing for me, as indeed work always is for everybody. The unemployed members of the household were probably discontented; at any rate, they seemed to be rather bored and rather cross when I saw them—but what could I do to help them? Trouble was assuredly in store for two, if not all four of us; still it was out of my power to avert that, and, luckily for me, it was also out of my power to brood over the future, except during an occasional spare five minutes.

Dukes, like the humblest mortals, have work to do, and their work, generally speaking, is not of a very interesting kind. Hurstbourne was disagreeably reminded of this on the following morning when the post brought him a request from the Mayor of a certain manufacturing town, situated some twenty or thirty miles north of us, that he would be pleased to open the public library which was about to be established in that prosperous borough. Another magnate had consented to perform that pleasing duty; but the other magnate was in bed with a dreadful bad cold, and his Worship appealed to his Grace's well-known kindness of heart to come over, at short notice, and to shed the requisite light of aristocratic patronage upon the proceedings.

"I'll see them all jolly well hanged first!" was Hurstbourne's first exclamation as he threw the document down. "What the dickens do I know about books and libraries? And what sort of a speech do they expect me to make, I wonder? I'll tell you what I'll do. I'll say I'm sorry I can't go, because—because I've got a bone in my leg, but that I'm sure my cousin, Mr Paul Gascoigne M.P., will be delighted to represent me on the auspicious occasion. How would that answer?"

Lady Charles didn't think it would answer at all. Lady Charles liked ceremonies, and could not approve of any plan which would have the effect of thrusting Mr Paul Gascoigne M.P., into a position of undue prominence. She said—

"My dear boy, I know it is a nuisance; but we shall make ourselves unpopular if we shirk these nuisances, and Mr Martyn will write out your speech for you."

Mr Martyn said,—"Thank you very much;" and Hurstbourne, with a growl, went on to peruse the remainder of his correspondence.

When there are women about, one ought to have one's letters brought up to one's bedroom in the morning. I don't suppose there is very much good in my saying this; still, should these words chance to meet the eye of any member of my sex who may be conscious of sufficient strength of mind to act upon them, I feel sure that he will live to thank me. What the eye does not see the heart does not grieve over, and the heart of every woman must needs be grieved if she be not informed of the contents of a letter the origin of which has been revealed to her by the stamped address upon the flap of the envelope. Now, Lady Charles had been the first to enter the dining-room, while I had been the second. Consequently, we were both aware that there was a letter from Lavenham for Hurstbourne, and that it was directed in a feminine hand. Lady Charles had shown it to me, inquiring whether the handwriting was Lady Deverell's, and I had replied that it was not. The inference was obvious.

So we were in a position to form our own conclusions when Hurstbourne, after reading that letter, said—

"Let's see; what day is it that they want me to open their beastly library? Oh, Thursday. H'm—well, I suppose I had better swallow the pill and go. Compose a suitable speech for me, Martyn, will you, like a good chap? Chuck in a good lot of classical allusions and tags of poetry and all that, you know. If one is to do the thing at all, one may as well do it properly."

I said I would do my best. I assumed, and so, no doubt, did Lady Charles, that Miss St George was to be present at the projected ceremony; but that we were both mistaken seemed to be proved by Hurstbourne's reply to the remark which his mother could not resist making, after an interval of expectation—

"You have heard from Lavenham, I see. What has Paul Gascoigne got to say to you?"

"Oh, my letter wasn't from him," answered

Hurstbourne, with a somewhat exaggerated air of indifference; "it was from Miss St George. She writes about a dog that I promised I would try to get for her. She and her aunt are going south in a day or two, so I'm afraid I sha'n't be able to execute the commission before they start."

All the same, he did contrive to execute it, and on the following Thursday we took a very handsome and well-bred little Halifax terrier to the station with us. In the interim I had composed a speech for my noble patron, which, I flatter myself, was really brilliant and scholarly, and I had not only compelled him to learn it off by heart, but had made him spout it out to me several times, with appropriate emphasis and gesticulation. He acquitted himself, upon the whole, fairly well, and I don't know what Nora, who attended one of our rehearsals, can have meant by saying that such a harangue, coming from the lips of the Duke of Hurstbourne, would have sounded quite as natural and even more impressive, if I had put it into blank verse. The truth, I suppose, is that my poor Nora was

feeling sore and savage; and everybody, I am
sure, will agree with me that the very last
weapon which a woman in that sad plight should
attempt to wield is irony.

Well, Heaven knows that I bore no malice,
nor did Hurstbourne (which was the worst of it),
and the whole four of us drove over to Lavenham Road, in our best clothes and an open
carriage, and spirits which were at least super-
ficially excellent. The terrier skirmished about
over our knees, and, as his antics gave us something to talk about, he was a welcome addition
to the party. It was understood, though I don't
think any actual statement had been made to
that effect, that he was to be despatched to
London by rail; still I may safely say that
it was no great surprise to any of us to recognise Mr Gascoigne's carriage outside the
station, or to encounter Lady Deverell and Miss
St George on the platform. For my own part,
I confess I was momentarily surprised on learn-
ing that the ladies were not bound for the
same destination as ourselves and that our
meeting with them was a mere coincidence,

due to the circumstance that the northward
and southward expresses happened to pass
through Lavenham Road within a few minutes
of each other. I should have been more than
momentarily surprised if I had believed in
the coincidence; but, of course, I preceived at
once that what I was looking on at was neither
more nor less than an assignation. Therefore,
after taking off my hat and grinning and saying a few words to which nobody listened, I
thought the best thing I could do was to conduct Nora across the line to the down platform,
leaving Miss St George to lavish endearments
upon her new pet and Lady Charles to exchange
bitter-sweet amenities with the other old woman.

Hurstbourne and Lady Charles joined us by-
and-by. They were just in time to step into
the saloon carriage which had been ordered
for us—nothing, I am sure, would have induced
Lady Charles to travel in an ordinary first-
class compartment, now that she was in some
sort a dowager duchess—and, if one of them
was not contented with the result of the interview which had just come to an end, the other

evidently was. Hurstbourne scarcely pretended that he had met Miss St George by accident; he only said that he was glad she liked the dog and that he believed he had secured as good a specimen of the class for her as there was in the market. Lady Charles was a trifle flushed and out of breath; she was in truth no match for Lady Deverell, being a simple soul and having a very modest opinion of herself, notwithstanding the respect that she entertained for her son's rank.

The perusal of the morning papers prevented us from interchanging many remarks during our brief transit, and, on arriving at the end of it, we were received with all the honour and pomp which we were entitled to expect.

Readers would probably not thank me were I to describe at full length a ceremony of which most of them must have only too often witnessed the parallel. It was a ceremony like other such ceremonies, and it was marred by no hitch, unless you could count as such Hurstbourne's unintentional ascription of an apothegm to Marcus Aurelius which should, by rights, have

been placed to the credit of a later wearer of
the purple. After all, it was near enough for
all practical purposes, and I don't doubt that,
when I subsequently took the liberty of pointing out his slip to him, he was amply justified
in retorting that nobody knew the difference
between one of those old buffers and another.
Having discharged our duties to the public
satisfaction, we were entertained at a truly
magnificent luncheon by the Mayor; after
which somebody presented Lady Charles with
a bouquet and there was, as a matter of course,
more speechifying. I had not coached Hurstbourne for a second oration, so that he used
his own words and achieved a success far greater
than I could have secured for him with my carefully rounded periods. He was not very discreet.
He dragged in politics, which he ought not to
have done; he had something to say about the
preservation of foxes, which was not altogether
appropriate to the occasion, and his style was
almost too colloquial to be reported *verbatim* in
the local newspapers; but he won the sympathy
of his hearers, who cheered him to the echo.

"His Grace," Lady Charles remarked to me, as we rose from the table, "thoroughly understands the art of dealing with his inferiors." She added, in case my mother-wit should not have enabled me to discover as much, that that was a most important art to have mastered in these democratic days.

The art of dealing with his equals may, perhaps, not have been one with the intricacies of which his Grace was equally familiar; or, possibly, I may be over presumptuous in claiming a place for myself and my sister amongst his equals. Either way, I don't think that he displayed conspicuous tact by holding forth to Nora, during our return journey, upon the beauty, the talents and the general distinction of Miss St George. Nor, to be quite impartial, do I think that it was wise on Nora's part to vie with him in extolling the merits of a lady whom she scarcely knew, and whom it was obvious to the meanest capacity that she detested. Lady Charles was compelled at length to take the part of the absent by remarking—

"Well, she is a handsome girl, but, if you

come to that, there are plenty of other handsome girls about. I don't see what she has
done that you should try to make her out
talented as well."

Nora, as I have intimated above, did not really
so consider her; but, for my own part, I thought
Miss St George had played her cards tolerably
skilfully, and I was confirmed in my opinion
by Hurstbourne's amazing assertion that she
was, at all events, "too talented, by long chalks,
for a useless duffer like that fellow Paul." Mr
Paul Gascoigne may have been a useless duffer,
but I was afraid I knew another individual
whom the description fitted equally well, and
who was in quite as great danger of being made
a fool of.

Well, if the poor, dear fellow was a fool
already, without need of anybody's interven-
tion, and if he couldn't see what was being
made as plain for him as plain could be, so
much the better! I took comfort from that
thought while my sister was betraying her
secret over and over again and escaping detection. After all, I should have hated Hurst-

bourne if he had been vain enough to detect
it, and I was not half as much provoked with
him as I was with her. I have often noticed
—and I daresay other people may have noticed
the same thing, though, to the best of my
belief, they haven't often said so—that women,
who are so infinitely more acute than we are,
are nevertheless far worse hands at keeping
their own counsel under certain circumstances.
They always adopt the same transparent sys-
tem of tactics, and the strange part of it is
that they don't always fail in misleading the
person whom it is their wish to mislead. As
for the bystanders, it is impossible that they
should be misled, unless they happen to be
as placidly dense as good Lady Charles Gascoigne, and one can't safely count upon meeting
with a large number of Lady Charles Gascoignes.

For all that, I could see that Hurstbourne
did not altogether like my sister's ready acquiescence in his eulogies of the girl who (as
she doubtless imagined) had supplanted her.
He was probably conscious of her insincerity,
though he could not understand why she

should be insincere—which naturally irritated
him. I need scarcely say that I was upon
tenterhooks the whole time, fearing lest he
should be enlightened by some unguarded utterance; and a very great joy and relief it
was to me to hear him announce, all of a
sudden, that he was going off to Leicester-
shire, at last, to finish the season.

"It's rather ridiculous to hire a house and
stables at Melton for the winter and never
use them," he explained, half apologetically;
though, indeed, there was not the slightest
reason to apologise.

I concurred promptly and cordially in his
sentiments, as did also the ladies, and I
believe that all three of us inquired at one
and the same moment when he proposed to
start. He did not seem to be in the least
affronted by our alacrity, but answered—

"Well, there isn't much time to be lost, and
if to - morrow won't be too soon for you,
mother, I'll just fire off a telegram to tell
them that they may expect us, and I'll see
about arranging for the removal of the horses."

"So we are going to get rid of those good people at last; how glad you must be!" I remarked subsequently to Nora; and perhaps it was not a very kind speech to make; though, as all the world knows, cruelty is sometimes kinder than kindness.

She looked me full in the face, and replied composedly—

"I am not glad at all; I am very sorry. You see, when I told you that I hoped they wouldn't stay long, I didn't know what good people they were."

I suppose she understood me, and I suppose she guessed that I understood her; but, for the moment, it seemed expedient to say no more. If plainer language was to be resorted to, there would be time enough for that after the disturber of our peace should have departed; for the present, my chief anxiety was that she should maintain her self-control, which might have been shaken had I forced her into making the most humiliating avowal that a woman can make.

It came within the range of my duty to

extort a humiliating avowal from Hurstbourne
that evening. I had to tell him that, unless
I were made more fully acquainted with the
state of his affairs than I had hitherto been,
it would be impossible for me to frame my
annual budget upon anything like sound fin-
ancial principles, and, after a good deal of
humming and hawing, he brought himself to
the point of making sundry revelations which
caused my jaw to drop. I had been pretty
sure that some such revelations were in store
for me; but I had not imagined that things
were quite so bad as they appeared to be,
and it was absolutely necessary to warn him
that he could not go on at that rate much
longer without being quite unequivocally and
decisively ruined.

He was a little impressed by the stern rebuke
which I thought fit to address to him; but only
a little.

"Oh, that'll be all right," he concluded by
saying: "don't you worry your sober old head
about it. Everybody is more or less in debt,
and so long as these rascals get the exorbitant

interest that they demand, it won't pay them to ruin me, you may be sure. Besides, I'm going to be awfully economical. Besides that again, I'm going to win a pot of money over the spring handicaps. Why, my. dear, good fellow, if nothing else would keep me from going to smash, I should be kept from it by the thought of Paul Gascoigne's triumph in my discomfiture."

"It would be hard to discomfit him and easy to discomfit you," I returned with a sigh; "but I suppose you are bent upon attempting the more difficult enterprise, and there isn't much use in cautioning you that you are almost certain to fail. If you would reflect connectedly for a matter of five short minutes, you would see that the game isn't worth the candle; only, of course, you won't reflect."

I can't think why people are so apt to laugh at me when nothing has been more remote from my intentions than to be funny; but Hurstbourne has always acted in that way, and he acted in that way now. He proceeded to throw a couple of sofa-cushions at my head, and so effected his escape.

"The next thing," said I aloud, when he had deserted me, "will be that he will engage himself to Miss St George, which will indeed be an economical measure! It's a poor consolation to know that she will indubitably throw him over as soon as she discovers that he has very little more than his title to offer her."

CHAPTER III.

THE MAGNANIMITY OF MR BURGESS.

HURSTBOURNE and his mother left on the following morning. They were both of them most cordial and friendly in their manner of bidding us farewell, and a good deal was said about my promise that I would entrust Nora to Lady Charles's care during the coming London season; but I need not say that I had no intention of parting with my sister; nor, as I could plainly perceive, in spite of her apparent acquiescence, had she any idea of profiting by the glittering opportunity offered to her. They drove off at last and, I daresay, forgot our existence before they reached the station, and I am free to confess that the Castle seemed very big and empty and dreary without them.

"*Rien n'est changé,*" Louis XVIII. is reported

to have said, when he was restored to his loving subjects, "*il n'y a qu'un Français de plus;*" and so it was with us and with our life. Nothing was changed; there was only one person (for the other hardly counted) the less; but units of course often stand for more than thousands, and that is why it is difficult to believe that *Louis le Désiré*, who was no fool, can have ever uttered so silly a speech as that ascribed to him under the guise of an epigram. As for my sister and myself, we tried to pretend that we enjoyed being once more alone and that we were going to resume the ways and habits which had sufficed for our contentment a short time before; but I don't think we kept up the pretence particularly well. I was always half hoping, half fearing that she would confide in me, while she, very likely, thought my manner dry and unsympathetic. It could not well be otherwise, now that we shared a secret which neither of us chose to allude to in words. On the third day I encountered Nora, just before luncheon, in the garden, whither I had betaken myself for a breath of fresh air, and I forgot how it was that we began to speak of Lady Deverell.

"Did she say anything to you about Mr Burgess?" Nora asked.

"Well, yes," I answered; "she said something, about him. I should have been glad to tell her that you were no longer engaged to him; but, of course, I couldn't do that without your permission."

"I suppose she said I had treated him badly, didn't she?"

"I believe that was the gist of her remarks. Anyhow, she didn't think you were leading the sort of life that a future country parson's wife ought to lead. She also had the kindness to inform me that people were chattering about your having taken up your residence here as the guest of a bachelor—which was sufficiently ridiculous, considering the rank of the bachelor in question."

"Utterly ridiculous," agreed Nora, with only a slight change of colour. "Still, she was quite right in accusing me of having behaved badly to Mr Burgess. I wish, with all my heart, that I could have behaved better to him; but I couldn't."

"Then why not tell him so, and have done with it?" I asked.

"Yes; I shall have to tell him so—there's no help for it. He isn't a bad man, though. I know you think he is; and, if it were in any way possible—but it really is not possible!"

"Never for one single moment did I suppose that it was," I returned rather impatiently. "Write to him to-day, and get the thing over. Depend upon it, you can break the sad news without breaking his elderly heart. It isn't as if you had inherited a comfortable competence, you know."

Nora sighed and made no reply, which caused me to feel that I had expressed myself too brutally; but it was expecting a little too much of me to expect that, with all my troubles and anxieties, I should have any commiseration to spare for Mr Burgess. Moreover, I was exasperated by the thought that my sister was about to break off her engagement with that old man, not because she had no

love for him—which, of course, she could not
have—but because she loved somebody else,
who didn't care a straw for her.

"Ah, if only I had inherited a comfortable
competence," she exclaimed presently, "then I
shouldn't be a drag upon you, and it wouldn't
be my duty to marry any man who was
willing to support me. Nobody could realise
more clearly than I that it is my duty to
marry Mr Burgess, and for the last few days
I have been trying to bring myself to the
point of doing my duty; but it's no use. I
can't do it, Phil, and I must confess to him
that I can't."

There were tears in her eyes, and she looked
so miserable that I ought to have said something kind and consolatory, instead of return-
ing, in surly accents—

"Well, well, you told me that before, you
know, and there's nothing more to be said
about it. All you have to do is to write and
tell him what you have told me."

She answered very meekly that she would
do so. I can't tell why she thought it neces-

sary to enter upon an elaborate vindication of
Mr Burgess's character, to which I lent an in-
attentive ear.

She was still engaged in extolling the worth
of one who had always seemed to me about
as worthless a member of the community as
a respectable parish priest can be when a fly
was seen to drive up to the front door, whence
presently descended a burly figure familiar to
both of us.

"Good Heavens, Phil, there he is!" ejaculated Nora, turning pale with consternation.

"And a very good thing too," said I.
"Lady Deverell has sent him here to ask you
what you mean by it; and in less than five
minutes you can give him the desired information. He will lunch with us; and after
luncheon I will leave you alone for five
minutes. Now mind, Nora, he has no right
to be inquisitorial or to demand reasons. One
reason is quite sufficient for him; and I do
implore you not to let him have more than
one. If you do, you will be sorry for it
afterwards."

The caution may have been superfluous and may also have been a little unfeeling; but I could not forbear from uttering it, and I had no time to be more explicit, because Mr Burgess was already advancing towards us across the lawn, holding out both his huge white hands. I got the left one, and dropped it immediately after it had touched mine. He profited by its release to place it upon the top of Nora's, which he held for some seconds in an affectionate clasp, while he explained to what circumstances the delightful surprise of his visit was due.

He had undertaken to conduct a mission in a northern parish for a very dear friend of his, he said — I wonder why parsons of his type always describe brother parsons as their "very dear friends,"—and he had only been obliged to come a little out of his way in order to give himself the pleasure of a short talk with us both. He would be very glad to lunch with us, and was very sorry that he had just missed seeing another very dear friend of his—Lady Deverell—who, he believed,

had been staying recently in our neighbourhood.

For the life of me, I couldn't resist asking
him whether he hadn't heard from her since
she had left Lavenham, and, as he was a
truthful man, he admitted, with a quick side
glance at me, that he had. Then we went
into the house together, Nora looking very
much like a prisoner who is conscious that
even a plea of guilty will not avail to miti-
gate the punishment due to crime.

I scarcely remember what we talked about
during a meal which the presence of the
butler and two footmen rendered more for-
midable than it would have been had we
ventured to dispense with their services, as
Nora and I usually did; but I remember
that the labour of keeping up conversation
fell entirely upon our guest and myself, my
sister hardly opening her lips from start to
finish. At the earliest permissible moment I
mumbled some excuse and fled into my den.
Mr Burgess had mentioned that it would be
necessary for him to catch the four o'clock

train, so that there was not a great deal of
time to be lost, and my earnest hope was
that he would hear all that it concerned
him to hear, if not within the prescribed
five minutes, at least within a quarter-of-an-
hour.

However, a good half hour had elapsed,
and I was debating whether I ought not to
emerge from my retreat and assume a more
active part in the proceedings, when a discreet tap at the door was followed by the
entrance of the rejected one. My first glance
at his face convinced me that he was by no
means inconsolable; but he closed his eyes
and tried to look very woebegone as he sank
into a chair.

"My dear young friend," said he, "I have
just received a severe blow, which, unexpected
though it was by me, has not been, I believe,
unforeseen by you. Whether I have been
fairly or honourably treated I leave it to
you to judge; I will only say to you, as I
have said to your sister, that I see no
alternative open to me but to bow to her

decision. I am grieved that such a decision should have been imposed upon her by events with which, perhaps, I am imperfectly acquainted; but I bow to .it."

Being—as I think was but natural—somewhat irritated by the man's manner, I replied that I really did not know what else he could do. I said it would be mere hypocrisy on my part to pretend that I had ever considered the match a desirable one or that I regretted its abandonment. It had in fact, in my opinion, been far too hastily arranged.

"So Lady Deverell thinks," sighed Mr Burgess. "She may be right; she generally is right, because she is always animated by the kindliest and most unselfish sentiments. Still, I own that the change which I can detect in your sister's whole mental attitude has saddened me. She seems to me to have set her affections upon things of this world, and I greatly fear that she will only find out her mistake when it is beyond the reach of remedy."

"At least," I remarked, "she hasn't set her affections upon you, Mr Burgess; and you, I suppose, are more or less a thing of this world. Let us be thankful that she has been preserved from one irremediable mistake, and perhaps it will be time enough to sadden ourselves about her when we are quite sure that she has made another."

I know that it was flippant and impertinent of me to address a man of double my age in that way; I know he had just cause for complaint, and I know he was, after his fashion, a conscientious sort of mortal. But I was so certain that he would have been less resigned to his fate if Nora had had a little money of her own that I couldn't help being rather rude to him. Besides, I didn't like his half-sneering insinuation, the responsibility for which, I had no doubt, belonged to Lady Deverell.

For the rest, he did not resent my impertinence. He shook his head, and looked down at his fat, white fingers, and said he

was very glad that he had nothing to reproach himself with in connection with the
trial which it had pleased Heaven to lay
upon him. He was likewise kind enough
to assure me that he blamed neither me nor
Nora and that he proposed to remember us
both in his prayers. Perhaps he thought
that we stood in need of being prayed for,
and perhaps, if he did, he was not very far
wrong. I humbly and penitently admit that
I am incapable of thinking or speaking
justly about such specimens of humanity as
Mr Burgess. There are plenty of much
worse specimens whom I can understand and
sympathise with better, but possibly that is
more my misfortune than my fault. In any
case, I had nothing further to say to him
which could be accounted worth my while to
say, or his to listen to; so, presently, he
departed to take up his mission work, and if,
after accompanying him to the door, I made
a face at him behind his broad back, it will
be conceded that I had a right to relieve
my feelings by making a face at somebody.

I showed a thoroughly amiable and contented face to Nora, whom I hastened to rejoin. "So, there is an end of that!" I observed. "I hope we may never do a worse day's work."

She smiled at me through the tears with which her eyes were dimmed. "I'm afraid it may turn out to have been a bad day's work for you, Phil," she answered; "but useless as I am, I must at all events make some effort to earn my own living now. The unfortunate thing is that there are so very few occupations open to a partially educated woman. There's nursing, and there's the Post Office, and there's art needlework; I don't know whether on could gain enough to pay for bread and butter by any of those employments at first; but I should think one might after a time. Do you suppose that Uncle John would give me house-room until I could see my way a little? He said that, if the worst came to the worst, I might write and ask him for shelter."

"The worst," I remarked, "hasn't yet come

to the worst, inasmuch as I haven't yet pro-
claimed my intention of casting you adrift.
I don't know what I have done to justify
you in assuming that I am an incarnate fiend;
but I do know that you will stay here and
take care of your forlorn brother until further
notice, unless you have made up your mind
to quarrel with him."

"I can't do that, Phil," she answered decisively; "whatever happens, I can't go on
living here. The truth is that Lady Deverell
was quite right, and that I ought never to
have come here. Of course she was right in
saying that a girl ought not to be a guest of
a bachelor; you yourself felt that, though
you won't admit it."

"Is it only in deference to the conventional
prejudices of Lady Deverell that you propose
to leave this house and apply for a berth in
the Post Office?" I inquired.

She looked at me for a moment, and then
answered abruptly: "No, it isn't only on
account of that. What is the use of pretend-
ing any longer, Phil, when you know it all?—

the whole sham and disgrace and humiliation
of it! It is horrible even to speak of such
things; but perhaps it is better to speak of
them once for all and *never* again, than to
go on shirking them. I have seen by your
face for a long time that you are disgusted
with me, and well you may be! You can't
be more disgusted with me than I am with
myself; but there it is! This miserable and
ridiculous and contemptible thing has happened to me, and I can't even be quite positive
that you are the only one who has discovered
it. Most mercifully, the Duke hasn't; and
I want you to believe, Phil, that it hasn't
happened through any fault whatsoever of
his. All he meant was to be kind and sociable:
he couldn't possibly foresee that I should
become the wretched idiot that I am. Please
don't say anything. There isn't anything to be
said. Only you will admit now—won't you?—
that it is out of the question for me to go on
living here."

I could not tell her that I thought she
ought to remain at Hurstbourne Castle, nor

could I wish her to do so; all I could say
was that I meant to make my home with her
and that, when she left, we would leave together. After all, my present appointment,
lucrative though it was, was not in every
way satisfactory to me, and even if I did
not obtain another immediately, we should
not starve. I don't think I said much more
than that, because I knew what it must have
cost her to speak out to me as she had done,
and that no conceivable remark could be made
upon the subject which would not pain her.

"My dear Phil," was her reply, "I would
rather beg my bread from door to door than
let you leave the Duke, and it isn't only for
your sake that I say so. He must have somebody to look after his affairs, and if you desert
him, he will make straight for the Bankruptcy
Court. I am very grateful to you for wishing
to sacrifice yourself and him in order to suit
my convenience; but I shouldn't be in the
least bit grateful if you were actually to do
anything so insane."

We argued the point for some little time;

but neither of us, I think, really shook the resolution of the other. However, I so far got the best of the argument that I obtained Nora's consent to a temporary prolongation of existing arrangements. Hurstbourne was not at all likely to revisit his estates for another six months, and during his absence there was no reason why she should not remain with me. That she was anxious to turn her back upon a place which must always be full of painful associations for her I could well understand; but I could hardly see my way to sparing her that degree of suffering. Rich people, when they are sick or sad, go abroad and travel; poor people must needs have recourse to other methods of living down sorrow. For rich and poor alike it is but question of time.

CHAPTER IV.

I COME WHEN I AM CALLED.

Is it the result of centuries of civilisation, or a mere vague, inherited instinct of barbarism that compels us to keep our troubles to ourselves and to mention them only at rare intervals even to those from whom we would fain have no concealment? North American Indians are said to be our masters in the exercise of stoicism, and the courage which we are inclined to associate with good birth is for ever cropping up in the most unexpected quarters. Be that as it may, there is a certain class of sorrows which cannot be discussed with comfort or advantage, and to that class my poor Nora's sorrow belonged. It was tacitly agreed upon between us that the subject must be a forbidden one; during our daily walks and rides we talked about every imaginable subject, except that of which we were both thinking. I am sure she knew that I would gladly have consoled her, had consolation been possible; while I, on my side, was only too well aware that she was not the less mortified and miserable because she kept up such a brave show of cheerfulness.

Everything went on as if nothing was the matter; only everything had lost its savour. The days had gone by for ever when the bare facts of existence and robust health and of having one another's company, as well as good horses to ride, had sufficed for our common contentment; in vain for us Nature set about that low annual awakening which appeals more to she young than to those who have seen many springs come and go; in vain the hedgerows broke into bud and the crocuses and daffodils made bright patches of colour in the borders; in vain the bitter east winds of March yielded to the sunshine and showers of April and the

new year (which ought, of course, to begin at
the vernal equinox instead of in mid-winter)
held out flattering promises of change. We
knew that the only change that was in store
for us was not going to be a change for the
better, and it was hardly worth our while to
maintain that elaborate affectation of jollity
upon which we expended such gallant efforts.
The present never forgives, and the past never
returns; do what we would, we could not be
what we had been a few short months before
—*ça n'etait plus ça.*

It was at this time that I composed a dozen
or so of those sonnets which, as a benevolent
critic afterwards remarked, had the ring of true
pathos. Other critics failed to detect that
quality in them, and upon dispassionate re-
perusal, I must confess that I fail to detect it
myself. But that is only because I am not
a poet. Had I been dowered with the gift of
putting my thoughts into appropriate language,
I must have been pathetic; for nobody could
have realised more clearly than I did the
tragic comedy of the whole situation. What,

indeed, could have been more tragi-comic than
that the life of such a girl as Nora should
be unwittingly spoilt by a commonplace, good-
hearted nonentity like Hurstbourne? It is true
that very few lives are really spoilt by one unlucky love affair, and I naturally hoped that
hers would not be; still, I almost believe that
the first love is the sole genuine one, and in
any case, there was little likelihood of her
making a speedy recovery.

Well, I had a sufficiency of prosaic matters to
claim my attention during the intervals of
poetic inspiration. I suppose the details of
Hurstbourne's gradual progress towards insol-
vency would not interest the reader as much
as they interested me; so I will not dwell upon
them. But I may mention that scarcely a day's
post came in without bringing demands upon
me which I could not meet without imprudence,
and that, as the days grew into weeks, it
became more and more evident to me that he
had plunged out of his depth. I wrote to him
again and again, asking him plainly at last
whether he wished to sink, since there could

be no doubt that his swimming powers must ere long be exhausted. Sometimes he answered and sometimes he didn't; he might have spared himself the trouble of answering at all, for such replies as he vouchsafed to me were not even remotely to the purpose.

"You ought never to have let him out of your sight," said Nora. I was so worried at times that she perceived my distress and made me tell her all about it. Women can always manage to do that with us, and I wish with all my heart that they couldn't. "You ought never to have let him out of your sight. You know what he is, and that he can't help doing what the people about him do, unless there is somebody at hand to put a salutary check upon him. As far as that goes, he knows it himself. I think, if you were a true friend, you would follow him up to London, Phil. You can't doubt that he would be delighted to welcome you."

I assured her that I could perfectly well doubt it, added to which, I had duties to perform where I was. Her suggestion struck me as eminently feminine and unpractical. It was no part of my avocations to cling to the tail of a donkey who was bent upon precipitating himself over a cliff, and so I told her. Yet, when in the beginning of May, I received a somewhat urgent letter from Hurstbourne begging me to run up to Berkeley Square for a few days, as he was anxious to consult me upon matters of business, I could not do otherwise than obey the summons.

"Now mind, Phil," was Nora's parting injunction to me, "you are not to hurry back on my account. I shall be very well taken care of by the servants, and you will probably find that the Duke is in much greater need of being taken care of than, I am."

That was a probability which was not to be contested, but I had little expectation of finding Hurstbourne in a mood to be influenced by any wise advice of mine; nor, as a matter of fact, could I induce him to listen for a moment to the statement upon which I embarked as soon as he had done telling me what pleasure it gave him to see me again and what a good fellow I was to have come so promptly when I was called.

"Yes, yes, my dear chap," he interrupted, "but I really haven't time to go into figures now. I must be off in a minute, and there are people coming to dinner, and after that I shall have to look in at half-a-dozen places. To-morrow morning, though, we'll have a palaver, and then you and the lawyers had better meet and try to muddle things out somehow among you. I'll be hanged if *I* can make head or tail of them."

For a few seconds he stood pinching his lower lip between his thumb and forefinger and looking a little glum; then he pulled himself together, glanced at his watch and hurried towards the door of the library in which he had received me.

"I can't stop," said he. "You'll make yourself at home and order what you want, won't you? Why didn't you bring Miss Nora? I wish you had. There's a room all ready for her, you know, as soon as she cares to come and occupy it; but my mother will arrange about that with you."

Lady Charles, when I went upstairs to pay my respects to her, was indeed more pressing in her kindly offers of hospitality than I could have wished her to be, and it was no easy task to make the excuses which had to be made. There was, of course, no ostensible reason why Nora should not come up to town at once. I could only fence this question by saying that perhaps she would come by-and-by, that she was a little out of sorts at present and scarcely fit to face much fatigue, and so forth. I daresay Lady Charles might have smelt a rat if she had not been the most unsuspecting of women, and if she had not been a good deal preoccupied with her own affairs and those of her son.

"I am afraid Arthur has been getting into difficulties," she said rather anxiously—her speaking of Hurstbourne as "Arthur," instead of "His Grace," was always a sure sign of mental disquietude on her part—" has he told you about them? No? Well, it isn't really serious, I hope; though he has been quite extraordinarily unfortunate with his horses so far."

"If he is in difficulties he must be persuaded to retrench," I observed.

"Oh, yes; I am sure he will do that, if necessary. But in the meantime he must live in a style befitting his rank, and it would be a great mistake to submit to the arrogance of Paul Gascoigne, who loses no opportunity of reminding people that he is the late Duke's heir. He has been entertaining as profusely and extravagantly as if he were some mushroom American millionaire, which, unluckily, is just the sort of vulgar self-assertion that succeeds in these days. Our purse is not long enough to compete with his; but at least we do mix in society as good as he can secure and perhaps a little more select. The Duke and Duchess of Saxe-Groschen-Pfennighausen are dining with us to-night."

That was indeed a legitimate cause for pride and gratification, and I had nothing to say in disparagement of it. I don't know that it costs more to entertain Royalties at dinner than to provide a similar repast for mere British commoners, nor would it have been at all beyond the Duke of Hurstbourne's power to feast Royal personages in that way, if only he had kept within his income in other respects. But, as Nora had too truly said, he could not help doing what those about him did, and the magnates of the turf are, I take it, for the most part, men of considerable wealth.

I had not the honour of sitting down to table with their Serene Highnesses. My evening repast was served to me in another room, with many apologies and full explanations of the inexorable laws of etiquette. Later on I was vouchsafed a glimpse of these exalted beings, as well as of other starred and ribboned individuals in the drawing-room. But Hurstbourne and his mother went off to some entertainment the moment that their guests had departed; so it was not until the following morning that I was enabled to enter upon matters of business and finance. Then I was closeted for half an hour with my patron,

and with a grave representative of the firm
of family lawyers, and then it was that my
worst apprehensions were more than confirmed.
Things were very bad indeed, and, as far as
I could see, were going to be worse. It was
not only that large sums had already been bor-
rowed and that mortgages were freely spoken-
of, but that there were heavy debts of honour
which must absolutely be discharged forthwith,
and which there was not anything like enough
money in the bank to defray.

"It just comes to this," I said at length,
"you may be tided over this crisis, but only
on condition that you enter at once upon
a strict course of economy, which will have
to be persevered in for several years to come.
If you haven't strength of mind enough to
face that necessity, nobody and nothing in
the world can save you from permanent ruin."

The man of law backed me up, though he
stated his views with rather more deference
and circumlocution; but Hurstbourne did not
seem to be greatly impressed by either of us.
He said we should have to do the best we

could, and that, if he was to come to grief,
he must come to grief.

"Anyhow, I'm not quite at my last gasp
yet," he added. "The luck must turn some
time, and, if there's any justice, I ought to
win a pot of money at Kempton Park, and
Manchester and Sandown. You fellows don't
understand that no man can race without
running risks."

I ventured to think that that was just what
we did understand, but he was not amenable
to the dictates of reason and common sense.
Afterwards he told me confidentially that it
was a sheer waste of breath to talk to him
about reducing his establishment and selling
his thoroughbreds at that particular juncture.
For various reasons the thing couldn't be done
just then without an immense pecuniary
sacrifice; added to which, everybody would
laugh at him if he were to show the white
feather so soon after having made a bold
start.

"And even if I didn't mind being laughed
at by everybody else, I couldn't stand

being laughed at by Paul Gascoigne. Do you see?"

I saw, and I said I was very sorry to see that he was such an unspeakable ass, whereat he burst out laughing. In replying to some further observations and questions of mine, he informed me that Miss St George was in London with her aunt and that he met her pretty frequently.

"It would do you good to watch Pauls sour face when I dance with her," said he. "Paul can do one or two things; he's a tolerably good speaker, I believe, and, of course, with all his money, he can give his friends a first-class dinner, but he can't dance, and Miss St George can."

I doubted whether it would make me much happier to look on at the spectacle alluded to, but, such as it was, I was privileged to witness it that evening, when Hurstbourne and Lady Charles kindly insisted upon dragging me to a ball at which Lady Deverell and her niece were also present. Hurstbourne's attentions to the latter lady were so marked that everybody noticed them. I suppose he must have intended them to be noticed. As for Mr Gascoigne, he certainly did look sour, and so, for the matter of that, did my esteemed friend Lady Deverell.

"So you have come up from the country," were the first words with which her ladyship greeted me. "You have been sent for, perhaps? Not that you are likely to do much good, if all that I hear is true. Have you brought Nora with you?"

I replied that I had not done so, as I had hoped only to be detained a few days in London. In answer to further interrogatories, I had to admit that my stay was likely to be a longer one than I had anticipated, where-upon Lady Deverell surprised me a little by rejoining—

"Then I hope you will let Nora come to me while you are here. You can't leave her at Hurstbourne Castle all by herself, and really, if you will believe me, Lady Charles Gascoigne is not the sort of chaperon whom your poor, dear mother would have chosen for her daughter.

May I write to Nora to-morrow, and tell her that you consent to my taking charge of her for a time? I am obliged to take my niece about, so that she need not be afraid of being dull, and I am sure you, on your side, must feel that she will be rather safer with me than with those people."

No doubt she would, although the obstacles which I saw in the way of her accepting hospitality from "those people" might not be precisely the ones alluded to by Lady Deverell. I was not quick-witted enough to guess why this old friend of ours was so anxious to assume the temporary guardianship of my sister. I thought she really meant to be kind, and I thought also that I might do a great deal worse than take advantage of her proferred kindness. It was evident to me that I should have to stay on in Berkeley Square. I was very uneasy about Hurstbourne, and did not want to leave him if I could possibly help it, yet supposing that I did stay, it would be almost impossible to resist the importunities of Lady Charles, unless I either told her the truth (which was

out of the question) or could plead as an
excuse that Lady Deverell, who, after all, had
provided my sister with a home when we had
been deprived of our own, possessed a prior
claim upon Nora's companionship.

Actuated by these considerations, I said,—

"Well, thank you; it is very good of you,
and I will write to Nora about it. I don't
know whether she is particularly ambitious
of coming up to London; but I am afraid I
shall not be able to return north yet awhile."

"That is all settled, then," returned Lady
Deverell, who appeared to think that the
assent of the person chiefly concerned was a
quantité négligeable. "She shall be made welcome, and I hope there is no necessity for me
to assure you that I shall be very careful to
avoid introducing her to anyone of whom
your mother would have disapproved. Of course
I am not responsible for her being already
acquainted with the Duke of Hurstbourne."

"I should never dream of being so unjust
as to hold you responsible for that calamity,"
I answered; "you can't even prevent your

own niece from dancing with the wicked Duke,
I observe."

I think Lady Deverell must have been deprived of her self-control by the episodes of
the evening, for, instead of snubbing me, she
said: "Leila is an obstinate, contradictious
fool!" Then she dived into her pocket, drew
forth a big pocket handkerchief and blew a
resounding blast upon her nose.

"Not," she resumed, after a pause, during
which she might have had time to reflect
upon the imprudence of her language—"not,
mind you, that I am in the least degree afraid
of your ducal friend. He is three parts ruined
already, and before this time next year he
will probably be residing at Boulogne or some
such place upon an allowance made to him
by his trustees. No; it is nothing to me
whether he dances with my niece or with
somebody else on the brink of a volcano.
You, I am afraid, are likely to suffer when the
crash comes; but that is only what I foresaw
and forewarned you of from the outset."

Not being ready with any adequate rejoinder,

I fell back and, shortly afterwards, effected my escape. Full well I knew that the crash was coming; perhaps it was a good thing, that, in view of its imminence, Nora should be furnished with an unamiable, yet useful and wealthy protectress.

CHAPTER V.

THE DOWN-HILL ROAD.

I WROTE to Nora, and, in the course of a few days, had a reply from her to the effect that she had received Lady Deverell's invitation and intended to accept it. "I am sure you are quite right to remain in Berkeley Square," she told me; "and for the reason that you know of, it wouldn't be possible for me to join you there. So I ought to be, and I am, very grateful to Lady Deverell for having helped me out of a difficulty. I don't exactly expect to enjoy myself with her, but I couldn't very well have stayed on here for an indefinite length of time without you, and I hope I am not quite much an idiot as you naturally take me for. I mean, I am capable of being amused and of conducting myself properly in fashionable society."

Fortified by these assurances, I proceeded to break the news to Lady Charles Gascoigne, who, as I anticipated would be the case, was not best pleased.

"I thought," she said, "it was an understood thing that your sister was to come to us. I must confess that I am surprised at her preferring to place herself under the wing of that horrid old cat, who doesn't really know anybody and who won't be able to take her to the best houses."

I humbly submitted that winged cats are *raræ aves* and that, if Lady Deverell belonged to that species, she might manage to achieve higher social flights than it had hitherto been worth her while to attempt.

"You see," I remarked, "she is now in charge of an ambitious niece, who will probably find means of admittance into the best houses. Besides, Nora is under obligations to her which can't be forgotten or set aside. I am sure you will admit that as readily as you will admit that one isn't always free to consult one's personal inclinations."

Lady Charles was too good-natured or, it may be, too indifferent to quarrel with us; but Hurstbourne, on being informed of the arrangement which had been made, with my sanction, astonished me by the vehemence of his protestations against it.

"I tell you frankly, Martyn," said he, "that I call it deuced unfriendly. If your sister doesn't care to come and stay with us, well and good; that is a question for her to decide according to her taste, and I wouldn't for the world urge her to enter this pandemonium against her wish. But, since it seems that she does want to see what a London season is like, I really think she might have established herself somewhere else than in the enemy's camp."

"Why will you persist in calling it the enemy's camp?" I asked. "What is the use of regarding people as enemies who haven't injured you, and who, as far as I am aware, have no intention of injuring you? Lady Deverell is upon visiting terms with your mother, you know."

Indeed, I had ascertained that a sort of ill-tempered treaty of peace had been concluded between these two ladies and that they shook hands when they met, although they would doubtless have preferred to scratch out one another's eyes.

"Oh, it isn't that," returned Hurstbourne; "I don't care a button whether old Deverell loves us or hates us, and she doesn't make much disguise of her hatred. I only call her the enemy because she is hand-and-glove with Paul Gascoigne, who is our enemy, if ever we had one. Moreover, I can't see why you should be so eager to thrust your sister into the degraded mob which goes by the name of London society; she would be a great deal better off and a great deal happier down in the country, where I wish to Heaven I was! However, I suppose neither you nor she will be deterred by anything that I can say."

I answered that I had no fear of my sister's being contaminated, but that I should sincerely rejoice if he would lend the force of example to such admirable precepts by quitting a society which he professed to despise and which was evidently becoming far too expensive for him. Thereupon he frowned, and grunted and went away. It was easy enough to put the poor fellow to silence by alluding to his pecuniary embarrassments, and it was not very generous of me to adopt that method with him; all I can plead is that it was necessary to shut him up somehow or other.

I went to meet Nora at the King's Cross Station, on her arrival, and drove with her to Lady Deverell's house in Upper Grosvenor Street. She seemed to be in better health and spirits than when I had parted from her, and she laughed as she implored me not to pull such a long face.

"I really am not going to die, Phil," said she; "my disease isn't a mortal one, as everybody is aware, and I shall be convalescent before you know where you are. I have brought a large supply of tonics with me in the shape of good resolutions, and I daresay Lady Deverell will kindly provide others in the shape of respectable, marriageable gentlemen.

So, if you please, we will treat bygones as bygones, henceforth and for ever."

"Very well," I answered — for in truth that appeared to me to be our wisest plan — "but the respectable, marriageable gentlemen aren't bygones."

"Only one of them. The others belong to the future, and when they belong to the present we will discuss them as much as you like. Not that we shall have much to discuss; because, if they are marriageable and respectable, nothing more will be required of them."

"Something more will be required of them by me," I remarked. "I don't suppose you mean what you say, Nora; but if, by any chance, you did, you would be rather inconsequent, wouldn't you? Why did you break off your engagement to Mr Burgess, pray?"

"Well—because he was Mr Burgess. Some people are impossible; others are perfectly possible, though they may not be the precise embodiment of one's romantic dreams. I know what you are thinking; but you are mistaken. I am not going to accept the first man who asks me out of pique, or in order to punish somebody to whom that would be no punishment at all; only it is obvious that I must either marry or become a burden and a nuisance to my nearest male relative. Consequently, I have made up my mind to marry; and cousequently I am now on my way to stay with Lady Deverell."

"Then," I returned, "all I can say is that I hope nobody will ask you."

"If nobody does, there will still remain the Post Office. Now let us talk about something else. Have you been to see a publisher yet? And if not, why not?"

"As a matter of fact, I had interviewed a publisher, and a very polite, as well as a very discouraging gentleman I had found him. But that is neither here nor there. It was of infinitely greater importance to me than all the literary fame or profit in the world that my sister should be restrained from committing some rash action, and I could not feel as sure as I should have liked to feel that she would be restrained by Lady Deverell, to whose care

I presently had the honour of confiding her.
I was puzzled by the old lady's amiability; I
could not understand her bland acquiescence in
the dismissal of her pet parson, nor was I able
to arrive at any comprehension of her motives
for showing us so much kindness. A desire on
her part to spite Lady Charles hardly seemed
to be a sufficient explanation of them.

"Of course you will want to see as much
as you can of your sister," she said very graciously, "and we are not far from Berkeley
Square, you know. One of the servants will
always be available to take her round there,
if you would rather she didn't walk through the
streets alone."

It seemed unlikely that Nora would wish to
pay frequent visits to Berkeley Square, but it
was certainly incumbent upon her to pay a
speedy visit to Lady Charles Gascoigne, and I
suggested that she might do so about half-past
five on the following afternoon. "When," I
was careful to add, for my sister's benefit,
"you may count upon finding Lady Charles
at home and all by herself. That is to say

that you will probably find me with her, because I shall make a point of being there;
but Hurstbourne seldom shows his face before
the dinner hour."

This was a strictly truthful assertion, though
Hurstbourne saw fit to falsify it. I mentioned,
iu the course of the ensuing day, that Nora
would be coming about tea-time, and I suppose
he must have taken note of my words, for no
sooner had she arrived, and been embraced and
scolded for her breach of faith with a lady
whose earnest wish it had been to have the
pleasure of introducing her into the highest
circles, than in he walked.

"I have a crow to pluck with you, Miss
Nora," he made haste to announce. "I should
like to know what you mean by turning your
back upon us and going over to the enemy.
Your brother won't allow that Lady Deverell
is the enemy; but you aren't such an old
humbug as he is, and I'm sure you won't pretend to think that she is a friend of ours.
So now, perhaps, you'll kindly explain yourself."

I was thankful to perceive that Nora's

emotions were well under control. She made much the same excuse as I had already made to Lady Charles on her behalf, and did not treat his remonstrances seriously. It may have been painful to her to meet him and talk with him, but she did not look as though she were in pain, and, after a time, I felt able to relax my vigilant observation of her words and ways. When we had finished our tea, Hurstbourne and she retired into the back drawing-room together, upon I forget what pretext, while Lady Charles entertained me with a protracted description of a garden party at which she had been present, and at which she appeared to have met quite a galaxy of celebrities.

"I had a long chat with His Royal Highness," the poor old thing told me, with irrepressible glee, "and he was as simple and natural as possible — just like any ordinary person. He said he couldn't think how it was that he had never met me before. His Grace is a great deal in that set now, you know,"

I had not the heart to distress her by saying

that his Grace's participation in the diversions of that set was likely to be a brief one. I allowed her to prattle on, and did not contradict her when she declared that a Duke of Hurstbourne possessed almost a prescriptive right to some post connected with the Royal Household.

"At present," she remarked, "all the appointments that he could accept are filled up, and the Tories are naturally reluctant to bestow any honour upon the head of one of the historic Whig houses; but I think they will find, when a vacancy does occur, that his claims are too strong to be resisted."

The head of the historic Whig house presently emerged from his retreat in the back drawing-room to inform us that Miss Martyn said she must be off, and that he proposed to see her home. Miss Martyn, however, declined his proffered escort, and, as it appeared that Lady Deverell's maid was waiting for her in the hall, he had to admit that she stood in need of no additional protection.

" I shall see you again before long, I hope,"

said he, as he shook hands with Nora at the foot of the stairs; "meanwhile, I'll endeavour to lay your good advice to heart. You won't go very far wrong, though, if you bestow an occasional thought upon mine."

"Yours wasn't much to the point," observed Nora; "mine was. Good evening."

It was within the range of my capacities to surmise what he had been counselling her to do and avoid; but, as I felt somewhat curious to learn the nature of her exhortations to him, I made so bold as to interrogate him upon the subject.

"My dear fellow," he answered, "your sister is almost as wise as you are—which is saying a good deal. She sees what you see, and what lots of people who aren't so wise as either of you see too. What she doesn't see, and what I can't explain to her, is that it's too late for me to make a fresh start now. The flag's down, we're all off, and I've got to ride the race out, whether I win or whether I come a bowling cropper. I don't say that the stakes were worth entering for; I daresay they weren't; and

I daresay I shouldn't go in for them a second time; but what's the use of talking about that at this time of day? I must do the best I can; and I mean beating Paul Gascoigne, if it's in any way possible to beat him—I don't mind telling you that much."

"In what way is it possible to beat him?" I inquired. "Not in politics, not in ostentation, certainly not upon the turf, with which he has nothing to do. Would you call it beating him to bind yourself for life to a woman who will hate you unless you can allow her an exorbitant sum in the shape of pin-money, and who, if you would only leave her alone, would make him quite satisfactorily miserable for the rest of his days?"

Hurstbourne seemed to think this an excellent joke, for he laughed loud and long.

"I never knew such a confirmed woman-hater as you are, Martyn," said he; "I don't believe you think there's a decent woman in the world, unless it is your sister. Miss St George is about as good as they make them — in an ordinary way of speaking. Besides, I haven't asked her to marry me yet; and I don't see why you should take it for granted that she will jump down my throat if I ever do."

I by no means took that for granted; on the contrary, I believed Miss St George to be far too wide awake to unite her fortunes with those of a man who had hopelessly compromised his own. What I did take for granted was that she would end by marrying Paul Gascoigne; though it seemed likely enough that she would amuse herself with Hurstbourne during the season—perhaps also utilise him as a stalking-horse.

It may be that, as time went on, I should in some degree have modified my ideas respecting her, had I seen her and Hurstbourne together more frequently than I did. Afterwards I heard from many people that her conduct had placed the fact of her being deeply smitten with him almost beyond a doubt, and indeed I suppose that the coldest and most calculating of women is not wholly exempt from the passions of love and jealousy. Miss St George—so I was subsequently informed—soon became violently jealous of my sister, who, of course, accompanied her and Lady Deverell to the houses which Hurstbourne was in the habit of frequenting, and whose intimacy with the Duke was fostered and encouraged in every way by her chaperon. Mr Gascoigne, meanwhile, was not less violently jealous of his cousin, so that, altogether, it must have been an amusing little comedy for those who were not personally interested in it to watch. I myself did not watch it, because I was only invited to a very few entertainments and declined most of the few invitations that I did receive. Neither Hurstbourne nor Lady Charles told me much about their social doings, while Nora was only careful to assure me that she was enjoying herself. She was a good deal admired, I heard.

Hurstbourne lost a considerable sum of money over the Derby. Somehow, or other, he was always managing to lose, and how he managed to pay I hardly knew. As far as I could see, it was only by means of most undesirable and costly devices that we were able to meet the current expenses of two large establishments. But it was useless to remonstrate with him, because he was possessed by the gambler's spirit, and clung to the gambler's last forlorn hope of setting himself straight by one brilliant and successful stroke. My poor dear Hurstbourne was, and is, one of the best fellows in England, and, like so many of the best fellows in England, he was bent upon committing moral suicide. I could not save him, though I was thoroughly ashamed of my ineptitude, if there was any consolation in that.

I need scarcely say that he had made arrangements for being present at every event of the Ascot meeting, and if these did not include the hire of a house in the neighbourhood of the course, that was only because I resolutely refused to provide him with the necessary funds. However, I could not prevent him from hiring a box, and I gathered that he intended the box to be tenanted not only by his mother, but by Lady Deverell and the two charming young ladies whose movements were supposed to be under Lady Deverell's control. It was with no little chagrin that he informed me one evening of the disappointment inflicted upon him by the rigid old chaperon in question.

"She says she don't approve of racing, and her conscience won't allow her to take her niece to a race-course," he grunted. "Did you ever hear such rubbish! I told her she needn't come unless she liked, because my mother would look after Miss St George just as well as she could, but she wouldn't give in; only she said she wasn't entitled to dictate to your sister, so I hope Miss Nora will join us. Miss Nora is such a good sportswoman that she's sure to enjoy herself ever so much more than we poor devils, who can't always afford to wish for the victory of the best horses, can expect to do. Besides, between you and me, I shouldn't be sorry to get her out of this hurly-burly for a bit. You choose to shut yourself up, and you don't see what's going on; but I tell you I don't half like this way in which some of these fellows are running after your sister. Old fellows, too, a good many of them, and she's inexperienced, you know, and there's nobody to give her a hint of caution, except that worldly - religious dowager. Ah, my dear Martyn, what a dog-hole of a world this is, and what asses we all are to live in the midst of it, when we might have lived outside of it and been healthy, and happy and jolly."

I was not much surprised when Nora declined to avail herself of the somewhat inadequate loophole of escape from the fashionable world offered to her by a visit to Ascot. She said that, although she might not be under Lady Deverell's orders, she was living in Lady Deverell's house, and ought to respect the prejudices of her temporary guardian; which sounded reasonable enough. Lady Charles went down on the Tuesday and Friday, and Hurstbourne dragged me with him, *faute de mieux*, on the other days. It was a disastrous business from start to finish, and when the meeting was at an end, he frankly confessed to me that matters were beginning to look devilish serious.

'They began to look devilish serious some time ago," I remarked with a sigh.

"H'm! I suppose they did; there's some comfort in that. Well, I may have better luck, and I think I shall, at Sandown, where I'm running a couple of my own horses. If that doesn't come off — but sufficient unto the day is the evil thereof. Did you see Paul Gascoigne swaggering about in the enclosure on Thursday?"

"No," I answered; "I didn't know that he was a patron of the turf."

"*He* a patron of the turf! Rather not! I suppose he went down partly because he thought it was the proper thing to show himself at Ascot on the Cup day, and partly because he hoped to witness my discomfiture. He wasn't disappointed there, but he hasn't bowled me out yet, I can tell him. I wish I knew what he meant by those everlasting insinuations of his that one can't take hold of. I'm pretty sure that he has got hold of some story, true or false, about my father; but if he holds a trump card, why doesn't he play it?"

"Perhaps," I suggested, "he is waiting to

see what card you mean to play. My belief
is that he won't trouble you if only you
won't interfere between him and Miss St
George, and it seems to me that you might
oblige him to that extent without any great
personal suffering or loss. Would you mind
telling me one thing, Hurstbourne; are you
really in love with Miss St George?"

"My dear old Martyn," answered Hurstbourne,
"I don't mind telling you anything in reason,
and nothing that you could say to me would
make me feel in the least bit huffy with you;
but—I put it to you now as a man and a
brother — don't you think that *is* rather an
impertinent question?"

CHAPTER VI.

NONE OF MY BUSINESS.

IT is generally accounted a creditable thing in any man that he should be a good loser, and the self-command which enables its possessor to meet disaster with a composed smile is, no doubt, a quality which deserves some admiration. Still, I must say that it was not a little provoking to a sober, commonplace person like myself to see my best friend diligently and cheerfully pounding his head against a brick wall. The wall was so evidently harder than his head that it was difficult to understand where the fun of the encounter came in, and I couldn't help saying as much to him.

"It is all very fine," I remarked, "to refrain from crying when you are hurt, but I really don't see why you should laugh about it."

"I laugh, my dear boy," he returned, "because I am not beat yet. When I am, we'll sit down on the floor, side by side, and stuff our fists into our eyes, if that will relieve your overcharged feelings. For the present, it won't do either you or me any harm to anticipate a victory at Sandown."

This was a few days after Ascot. Things had come to such a pass that no victory, at Sandown or elsewhere, was likely to set him upon his legs again, but perhaps, when a condemned man has started for the scaffold, it is a matter of small consequence whether he exhibits an edifying dejection or disappoints spectators by looking as if he didn't care. As for me, I perceived that my functions must soon come to an end. My daily routine work had ceased to possess any interest for me, now that the saving of a few pounds here and there could not affect the ultimate result one way or the other. I daresay that was why I hurried through it on that particular morning and, for no reason except that I did not know what else to do with myself, strolled off to Hyde Park.

I have always abhorred London, and it has always been incomprehensible to me that people who might be breathing fresh country air should deliberately choose to spend the best part of the summer in that thickly populated desert of bricks and pavement. But I don't wonder that the poor deluded creatures should be thankful for such an apology for green leaves and such an imitation of what flower-beds ought to look like as the park can afford them, and to my mind they look rather better and happier there than they do by candle-light. That is, the men and a few of the women look better; the majority of the latter have, of course, seen fit in these days to adopt a species of complexion which is ill-fitted to cope with the warm glow of a sunny June morning. I was wandering along, taking half-conscious notes of the passers-by as I went, and inwardly wondering who could have been the first extraordinary individual to suggest that mauve is a becoming colour to lay thickly upon human cheeks and chins, when I caught sight of Hurstbourne riding with Miss St George. There

was a groom behind them — Lady Deverell's
groom, I presumed, since he did not wear the
Gascoigne livery—but they were otherwise un-
accompanied and unattended, which seemed
rather imprudent on their part, unless they
wanted to be talked about. But very likely
one of them did, while the other didn't mind.
A man with whom I was slightly acquainted
took me by the elbow before I had ceased to
gaze at their backs, and said,—

"Does that really mean business? You ought
to know."

"Ought I?" I answered. "Well, I don't. It's
none of *my* business, anyhow."

"Oh, but I thought you were acting as a
sort of male nurse to the Duke. It's too bad
of you if you aren't, for nobody stands in
greater need of a nurse than that misguided
young man does. To live at the rate of about
three times your income is silly enough, but
you may take my word for it that that isn't
half so silly as marrying Miss St George. I
know, because my sister was at school with
her, and the girl is mother of the woman, as

Shakespeare or some other equally sharp-witted old quilldriver observes. Miss St George has no money, precious little brains and a beastly temper. If you have any influence over that unlucky Duke of yours, it is your duty to exert it and get him to drop this game, whatever other games that he doesn't understand he may insist upon playing."

"I have no influence over him to speak of," I replied rather crossly, "and I think Miss St George has brains enough to refuse a man who is spending three times his income—supposing Hurstbourne to be such a man. Added to which, Miss St George has a vigilant and competent aunt."

Then I turned and walked away, not caring to listen to any more remarks of the above description. I walked straight to the house of Miss St George's aunt; not because I wanted to see that lady, but because I did rather want to see Nora, to whom I had something to say. The chances were that before the autumn I should find myself free and unemployed; she also would, I hoped, be similarly situated; and it seemed to me that the time had nearly come for us to make some arrangement respecting the future.

Miss Martyn was at home, I was told, on reaching Upper Grosvenor Street, and very glad Miss Martyn was to see me. So, at least, she said; though she might have given a more flattering reason for her gladness.

"I was just wondering how I could manage to get a word with you, Phil," she began. "I want you to tell me whether all these things that people are saying are true. I can't ask anybody else, because I don't like to appear inquisitive; besides, I suppose all they could do would be to repeat hearsay. But *you* must know whether it is a fact or not that he has lost such enormous sums of late."

I did not think it worth while to waste time and breath by inquiring who "he" might be.

"It is a fact," I replied, "that he lost a good deal of money at Ascot. I can't tell you how much, and I don't know that it particularly signifies. It is just wildly possible that before the end of the racing season he may recoup himself for his losses; but I have given up all hope that he will ever consent to square his expenditure with his revenue; so, since the break-down must inevitably occur sooner or later, it may as well come in a few months as next year or the year after. For several reasons, in fact, the sooner it comes the better I shall be pleased. The sooner it comes the more likelihood there will be of our saving enough out of the wreck for him to live upon; though not enough, I trust, to tempt Miss St George, with whom I saw him riding in Rotten Row just now."

Nora looked very grave at this.

"Was he riding with her?" she asked. "If Lady Deverell hears of that she will be furious. As it was, there was very nearly a quarrel at breakfast time, because Miss St George insisted upon going out with the groom, and it did seem odd that she should be so determined to do what she had never cared to do before. They must have been seen together, of course."

"Oh, they must have been seen together," I agreed. "They must have been seen by several hundreds, not to say thousands, of persons besides your humble servant. But that is rather more Miss St George's look-out than yours or mine, isn't it?"

Nora made no immediate reply. She had received me in a small room—so small that it ought, perhaps, rather to be described as a recess of the drawing-room, from which it was separated by looped-up curtains and by one of those perforated cedar-wood screens wherewith the army of occupation in Egypt has flooded the abodes of its friends at home. While we were talking, she had been arranging cut flowers in a multitude of bowls and specimen-glasses, in preparation, I suppose, for a dinner-party, and she silently pursued this employment for some time before she said—

"I am afraid you will think I am jealous of Miss St George, Phil; but you will be mistaken if you do think so. I have quite got over my —my trouble now, and it isn't on that account —of course it *couldn't* be!—that I wish we could save him from her."

"She will save him and herself at one and

the same time," I answered. "It will be a case of *sauve qui peut* before long, and unless I am very much mistaken in the young lady, she won't be slow to join in the general flight."

"You say that," observed Nora, "because you neither understand her nor — nor the whole position of affairs. I don't believe she cared a bit for him when she was at Lavenham; she may have thought there was no harm in having a second string to her bow, or perhaps she may have been flattered by his admiration. But I am certain that she does care for him now; and it is almost entirely owing to Lady Deverell's mismanagement that she does."

"If she cares for him enough to marry him upon a mere pittance, she is entitled to our respectful sympathy," said I; "but I venture to doubt whether her aunt will be guilty of such gross mismanagement as to let her incur a sacrifice of that heroic description."

"I am afraid she is foolish enough to marry him," answered Nora. "I am sure she doesn't care for him enough to put up with any privations for his sake; and—she isn't at all afraid of her aunt. You won't understand unless I tell you all about it, and even when I have told you, the chances are that you won't believe the truth. However, here it is for you in all its nakedness. Lady Deverell, of course, has wanted all along to make up a match between her niece and Mr Gascoigne ; that much you must have seen for yourself. After a time she became alarmed by the Duke's attentions ; so she sent for me. Perhaps you didn't trace any connection between cause and effect there."

I confessed that I had failed to do so, and Nora went on—

"So did I until the scheme was made too apparent to mislead an infant. The Duke was supposed to have been more or less captivated by my charms down in the country—such a thing wasn't impossible, although, as you know, it didn't actually occur—and it was hoped that my sudden appearance in London would produce a certain effect upon him. The queer part of the business is that, instead of having produced that effect upon him, it has produced a rather startling effect upon some-body else. Naturally, he has talked and danced a good deal with me—we were always good friends, you know—and the consequence has been that his flirtation with Miss St George has become a serious love-affair. It was serious on his side from the first, I suppose, and now it is serious on hers. If, as you say, and as everybody says, he is upon the brink of ruin, his friends ought to do all they can to prevent him from making ruin more ruinous than there is any need for it to be by sharing it with Miss St George? Don't you think so?"

"Upon my word, I don't know," I replied rather snappishly. "Hurstbourne isn't the only person in the world who interests me, and, as I told you before, I have great confi-dence in Miss St George's distaste for heroic sacrifices. I may be wrong; but what strikes me most forcibly in all this is that I have some little right to resent your having been made a catspaw of. Do you yourself feel no sort of resentment, may I ask?"

"That isn't the question," said Nora. "Well,

since you ask me, I may as well admit that I do. The position is not a very dignified or a very agreeable one, and I haven't yet told you the worst of it—the worst, I mean, so far as I am concerned. All's fair in love and in war, and I don't very much wonder that when the Duke saw, as he couldn't help seeing, how things were, he should have taken advantage of his opportunities. He might have remembered that some trifle of consideration was due to me; but then, to be sure, he wasn't aware of my susceptibility. To speak plainly, he has chosen to enrage Miss St George of late by a rather conspicuous pretence of devotion to me. Well, it suited his purpose to make believe, and I forgive him, though I can't say that my personal affection for him has been exactly increased by his conduct. Still, I like him well enough to wish to do him a good turn if I can, and that is why I was anxious to hold a consultation with you."

"I also was anxious to hold a consultation with you," I answered; "but not about Hurstbourne. Let him go to the—well, let us

say to the dogs, since he seems to have set
his heart upon arriving at that destination. I
have done all I could for him; it is high time
that I began trying to do something for my
sister. And a man who has used my sister
as he has used you really mustn't expect me
to care particularly whether he and Miss St
George and the whole lot of them together
go to the dogs or not."

"Nevertheless, you do care," remarked Nora
quietly.

"Very well, I do care, if you will have it
so. But I care a great deal more for you than
I do for him; and there's nothing discreditable
in that statement, I hope.

Then I proceeded to unfold my plans. I
said I had resolved to resign my present post
and that, even if I wished to retain it, I
should not be able to do so much longer,
because Hurstbourne's affairs must soon be
placed in the hands of trustees. I propose to
take a small house somewhere on the outskirts
of London while looking about for some fresh
field in which to employ my energies, and I

added that Nora would have to make her home with me until she married. I went on to state that I did not ask her consent to this arrangement, seeing that I held myself justified in issuing commands upon the point, and she seemed to be much amused by the peremptory tone in which I informed her that I should permit no matrimonial alliance on her part, save one of affection.

"Poor old Phil!" she said, "how do you suppose that you can prevent me from accepting the first benevolent old gentleman who asks me? Two of them have already honoured me by offers. I seem destined to captivate elderly admirers."

"But you have refused them?" I said apprehensively.

"Oh, yes; I have refused them both—more shame for me! Nothing is so immoral or so deteriorating as to make resolutions and then break them for want of a pinch of courage. But never mind me just now; my prospects cn be discussed any day during the next two or three months, and so can yours. We have no time to lose, though, if we want to preserve the Duke from—"

Her sentence was interrupted by the abrupt throwing open of the drawing-room door and the entrance of two persons who were apparently in the midst of a heated altercation. Through the apertures of the carved screen I could see Miss St George in her riding-habit, and the angry face of Lady Deverell; but neither of the ladies saw me; otherwise, I am sure that the elder would not have said, in a loud, clear voice—

"It is nonsense to pretend that you have not deceived me, Leila, because you now admit having met him. If you had told me before you started that you were going out on purpose to meet him, you might claim to have behaved honestly."

"Only then you wouldn't have let me go," Miss St George observed.

"Most certainly I should not. Good gracious, Leila, can't you understand that you are making yourself perfectly ridiculous, besides endangering your chance of marrying really well? I

can assure you that you will never marry the
Duke of Hurstbourne, because I shall take
measures to prevent that if you drive me to
employ them, but my firm belief is that he
won't propose to you. Are you so blind as
not to see that he has lost his heart to poor
little Nora Martyn? I don't say he will make
a duchess of her—that would be too absurd,
although the poor child may be silly enough
to fancy that he will."

I confess that I should have been in honour
bound to sneeze before that if I could have
managed it, but it takes a few moments
to get up a thoroughly natural and effective
sneeze. Under cover of the tremendous hulla-
baloo which I presently succeeded in raising,
Nora made good her escape, while I stepped
smilingly forth from my ambush to face the
disconcerted ladies. They must have felt disconcerted, and one of them looked so; the
other, I am forced by the veracity incumbent
upon a conscientious historian to admit, did
not. Miss St George had one of her usual
vague nods at my service, and, as usual, gave

me to understand that my value in her estima-
tion, whether as a visitor or as an eavesdropper,
amounted exactly to zero.

"If you haven't anything more to say just
at present, I'll go upstairs and change," she
remarked to her aunt, and so left me to receive
Lady Deverell's apologies, of which I was not
defrauded.

Lady Deverell was ashamed of herself, and
admitted as much with a candour which disarmed attack.

"People have no business to hide behind
screens, and listeners hear no good of themselves," she continued, "but I am very sorry
that you overheard what I said just now.
Nevertheless, it was the truth, you know."

"The truth that Hurstbourne has lost his
heart to Nora, but that it would be too absurd
to credit him with any intention of marrying
her?" I asked.

"Oh, well, of course I shouldn't have used
those words in speaking to you, but if you
are not aware of the facts you really ought
to have been aware of them."

"Such is my density," I replied, "that what you call facts have remained, and still remain, unacknowledged by me. Supposing them to be facts, they make you out a trustworthy sort of chaperon, don't they?"

Lady Deverell sat down and began to defend herself against accusations which I had not made.

"It is all very well to abuse me," said she, "but I have done the best I could, and it happens to be my duty to take care of my niece as well as your sister. I don't see that I am to blame for having taken a little advantage of that young man's infatuation. If Nora had taken a fancy to him it might have been different; but she hasn't."

"How do you know that?" I inquired.

"I have eyes and ears, I have seen her with him and heard a good deal of what she has said to him. Like other girls, she thinks it a fine thing to have captivated a Duke, but I really don't believe that she would marry him, even if he were to propose to her. It is only fair to Nora to say that I have always recognised her keen sense of right and wrong."

"I wish," I remarked, "that yours were equally keen. It is only fair to myself to say that I consider you a most immoral old lady."

"Very well," returned Lady Deverell, with a short laugh; "under the circumstances, you are entitled to be rude, and we won't quarrel over it. I know you don't like me, and, frankly speaking, I don't much like you; still, I am not quite so bad as you suppose. I wouldn't place Nora's happiness in jeopardy even for the sake of that tiresome and perverse girl, Leila; I have profited by the course of events, that is all.

I had never liked Lady Deverell so well as I did at that moment. She was really an immoral old lady; but her fighting instincts were those of the good old race to which she belonged, and if she could only have made up her mind to cast aside all affectation of being religious, she probably would have not been a worse member of the community than other dowagers. We concluded a sort of armed truce, and she begged me not to make mischief by repeating to Nora a fragment of conversation which had never been intended to reach my ears. I thought it unnecessary to mention that the screen which had concealed me at the time had likewise concealed my sister.

I was walking down St James's Street, on my way to lunch at the Club, when I encountered Hurstbourne, who stopped me in order to say excitedly—

"Look here, old chap, I'll give you a real good tip for once. Back 'Mock Turtle' for all you're worth. He can't lose, and I can get you two to one even now."

I shook my head and declined the tempting offer. I know very little about racing; but I was dimly aware that "Mock Turtle" was one of the horses that Hurstbourne had bought with their engagements and that the animal was entered for some race or other in the forthcoming Sandown meeting.

"Have *you* backed him for all you're worth?" I asked.

"That wouldn't be much, would it?" he laughed. "I've backed him pretty heavily, though, and I've backed 'The Crocodile' too for the other event—which isn't an absolute certainty, I confess." He paused for a moment, tapping his boot with his cane and gazing down the street. "By the way," he resumed, "you're coming with us to old Mother Deverell's hop next Thursday, aren't you?"

"I shouldn't think I was," I answered; "as far as I know, I haven't been invited."

"Of course you have been invited, and of course you'll have to come. These two blessed races will be over by then, and I shall know better how I stand than I do now."

I don't know whether he meant me to infer that if "Mock Turtle" won, he would take that opportunity of proposing to Miss St George. He looked as if he wouldn't mind being questioned —which, I daresay, was why I abstained from questioning him. I was out of all patience with him, and that is the truth. Perhaps I was out of patience with Nora, and with Lady Deverell, and with myself, to boot. There are moments when the ridiculous and uncalled-for contrariety of things is too much for the patience even of a man who is at once prosaic and a poet.

CHAPTER VII.

HURSTBOURNE HAS MANY WARNINGS.

I HAD the effrontrey to call myself a poet in the last paragraph of the last chapter, and I don't know that my presumption was any the more excusable because I qualified it by the statement that I was a prosaic poet. I hasten to substitute the assertion that I am—or at least once was—a prosaic rhymester, which is a more intelligible definition than the other. What, I have sometimes wondered, are the constituent qualities of a true poet? I am not going to admit that facility of expression is one of them, because that may be acquired, readily in some cases, slowly and painfully in others, by everbody, just as everybody may learn to play the piano after a fashion. But I suppose that one essential attribute of the true poet is a certain insight into the by-ways of human

nature which can never be learnt by the majority of his fellow-creatures, though many of
them may be quite as well able as he to dis-
tinguish black from white, and A from B. Had
I been gifted with as much of that faculty as
was required for reading the not very recondite thoughts of such persons as Nora and
Hurstbourne and Lady Deverell and Miss St
George, I should, doubtless, have felt less per-
turbed about them all than I did; but the more
I reflected the more uncertain I became as to
what they would be at, and this naturally rendered me downhearted, as well as a trifle cross.
Moreover, the control of events seemed to have
been absolutely removed from my hands; so
that, like a weary play - goer, I was chiefly
anxious to reach a foregone conclusion, to see
the curtain fall and have done with it.

The fall of the curtain was not unlikely to
take place in Sandown; but I declined to accompany Hurstbourne thither, pleading, as an
excuse, that I was not a member of the Club
and that I preferred, for choice, to escape the
contumely with which outsiders are treated on

that exclusive pleasure-ground. Lady Charles
also for once decided to remain at home.
It was a very hot day, and she was tired, she
said. She certainly looked so. Probably it
had at length dawned upon her that her son
had made a stupendous fool of himself, and,
for all I know, she may have begun to realise
that she herself had been in a large measure
to blame for his folly. It did not really signify,
because the milk was spilt, and there was no
more use in crying over it than there was in
snapping at me. She did snap at me when
we met at the luncheon hour—it was not often
that she behaved in that way, poor good-natured
soul!—and I will not deny that I snapped back
at her. If our nerves were on edge, and if
we both expected to hear of a catastrophe before dinner-time, we had no great cause to feel
penitent or to ask pardon of one another.

However, that good Lady Charles's conscience must have been tenderer than mine, for
about six o'clock she sent to beg that I would
come downstairs and have a cup of tea with
her, and when I appeared, in obedience to her

request, she apologised, a little awkwardly, yet quite sufficiently, for having been rude to me earlier in the day.

"To tell you the truth, Mr Martyn," said she, "I am not happy about his Grace. I am afraid he is spending more money than he ought."

"There is no doubt about that," I replied; "I have been warning him that he was doing so for a long time past, but I can't do more than warn him. I wish it had occurred to you to do as much a little sooner."

She sighed, and remarked, with a queer mixture of regret and complacency, that I perhaps didn't understand the hereditary tendency of the family.

"The Gascoignes," said she, "have been generous and open-handed from time immemorial. His father was just the same, and so, I must say, was the late Duke, although— But, at all events, such is the family disposition, and it isn't a disposition to be ashamed of, after all."

"It is a disposition which requires to be supported by large revenues," I observed. "Mr

Paul Gascoigne appears to have obtained the revenues and escaped the generic taint."

"Well, you wouldn't wish Arthur to resemble him, I should hope."

"No—except in respect of income. But as you and Hurstbourne are agreed in despising him, why are you so desperately bent upon rivalling him? I believe two-thirds, if not the whole, of these embarrassments are due to your insane attempt to pit a poor man against a rich one on the very field where the rich man is sure of ultimate victory."

"Not at all," returned Lady Charles, with some animation. "Fight him we must, and Arthur is quite right to fight him; but it isn't only by spending as much money as he does that we hope to show him that he is not invincible."

"The common household flea," I ventured to remark, "is not invincible; yet one doesn't expend one's life and one's fortune and any little intelligence that one may possess in stooping to conquer him. A simpler and a better plan is to avoid his haunts."

I should, doubtless, have proceeded to the utterance of further indiscretions, had not my oration been cut short by the entrance of Hurstbourne, who bounced into the room, with a radiant countenance and a pair of field-glasses slung over his shoulder, to announce that "Mock Turtle" had proved worthy of the confidence reposed in him by his backers.

"It looked like a near thing," he told us; "but the horse really won as he chose, and I believe the poor old Crocodile would have about won his race too, if he hadn't been a bit unlucky. Well, one mustn't be greedy; it's something to have pulled off the big event, isn't it?"

He was so elated that I had not the cruelty to inquire what might be the exact pecuniary result of having pulled off the big event, nor did he volunteer any more mercenary details for our benefit. The nearest approach that he made to a statement bearing upon that point was when he remarked exultingly—

"This will be a rare sell for Paul Gascoigne. He was going about all over the place yester-

day telling people that I was broke and pre-
tending to be deeply afflicted. He'd be afflicted
without any pretence if he knew how many
thousands more to the good I am this evening
than I was when he spoke."

So we gave ourselves up to triumph and
mutual congratulation, and it was not until the
next morning that I took leave to beg for more
specific information. It then appeared that
Hurstbourne really had won a rather large sum
of money in bets; the stake did not seem to
have been worth very much. Whether his success
was a thing to rejoice over or not depended
entirely upon the view that he might take and
the use he might make of it. It would be of
no sort of service to him or anybody else if it
only enabled him to go on living in the same
way for a few more months; and this was what
I strove to impress upon him, while we were
driving together in a hansom towards the City,
where we had some business to transact with
his lawyers.

"Well, hang it all, Martyn!" he exclaimed
reproachfully, "it's better to have won than to

have lost; you'll allow that, surely! What a dogged old wet blanket you are!"

"I shouldn't always be a wet blanket if the chimney wasn't always on fire," I returned; "it's worth while to maintain that unpleasant character, if I can prevent the house from being burnt down."

"Ah, but can you? Why not be jolly until the conflagration sets in? It's bound to come, I expect, and we're prepared for it—my mother and I. I daresay we shall manage to make ourselves tolerably comfortable among the ashes it won't be an altogether novel experience to us, you see. Anyhow, we can't be prudent and penurious until we're forced to be so; we aren't made that way."

"There is no accounting for tastes," I sighed "and if it were only a question of you and your mother—"

He understood my delicate allusion, for he laughed and declared that it wasn't yet a question of anybody else. To be sure, it *might* be, because there was such a thing as disinterested affection, although, of course, a fellow whose mind was so warped by unreasoning hatred of women as mine was wouldn't believe it. He did not, he made haste to add, flatter himself that he had inspired any woman with sentiments of disinterested affection.

"I wouldn't, if I were you," I responded drily; "such an illusion as that would be liable to be rudely dispelled from one moment to another."

The idea of Miss St George manifesting disinterested affection by taking up her abode upon a cinder heap with the man of her choice was really a little bit too comic.

Our conference with the lawyers had a somewhat sobering effect upon Hurstbourne, who, I take it, did not want to be reduced to downright poverty, and who, notwithstanding his brave words, probably did not believe altogether in the imminence of such a melancholy event. We agreed to walk home, and, as we paced along the Embankment, I talked to him with a seriousness which he professed himself able to appreciate.

"Only, you know," said he, "I can't begin cutting things down to-morrow. Let's get to the end of the season, and then we'll see. I suppose you won't understand what I mean; but it's a sort of point of honour with me not to cave in to Paul Gascoigne."

I confessed my utter inability to understand what Mr Gascoigne had to do with his cousin's annual expenditure, whereupon Hurstbourne burst out laughing and declared that it wasn't a bit of good to argue with a man who was "so beastly literal."

Doubtless he was right. Nothing could be gained by argument when the real premises were not before us, and I could only hope that Miss St George, who was far more competent to undertake the task than I, would ere long convince him of the vanity of his ambitions.

By the time that we had reached Whitehall we had abandoned the subject of finance. We were progressing along that thoroughfare, keeping up a desultory conversation upon topics of general interest, when whom should we encounter but the very insufficient fount and origin of all our woes. Mr Gascoigne was evidently on his way towards Westminster, and

looked the earnest legislator all over, with his
unbuttoned frock-coat and his neat umbrella,
which he carried over his shoulder in imitation
of a distinguished statesman with whose policy
he seldom finds himself in accord. Nothing, I
should think, can possibly prevent Mr Gascoigne
from becoming Chancellor of the Duchy of
Lancaster some day. He was in plenty of time,
and that, no doubt, was why he condescended
to pull up and shake hands with us both.

"Well, Arthur," said he; "you were lucky
for once at Sandown yesterday, I am glad to
hear."

"I won one race and lost another. I didn't
do badly on the day," answered Hurstbourne.
"I don't know why you should be glad to hear
of it, though."

"I am always glad to hear of your having
been successful," was Mr Gascoigne's bland rejoinder. "I only wish you gave me more frequent occasions for rejoicing on that score."

"Oh, I'll make you rejoice once or twice yet
before I die," retorted Hurstbourne grimly.

Hurstbourne is as pretty a fighter as any-

body could wish to see, but he requires the
fleuret de combat. He doesn't excite admiration
when the buttons are on the foils.

My eyes were upon Paul Gascoigne's face, and
for one instant I saw him look very nasty indeed; but he knew how to control himself, and
it was in his customary tone of composed affa-
bility that he said—

"You are going to Lady Deverell's ball to-
night, I suppose?"

"Yes, I am," replied Hurstbourne curtly. "Are
you?"

"I hope so. I may be detained rather late
in the House, but I shall try to put in an appearance during the course of the evening.
Lady Deverell and Miss St George kindly made
such a point of my being there that I mustn't
break faith with them."

Hurstbourne hailed a passing hansom and
jumped into it. Unlike his cousin, he had little
or no self-control, and I think he often ran
away, as it were, from his temper, fearing lest
it might lead him into doing or saying something that he might afterwards regret.

"Are you coming home, Martyn?" he called out.

"Not just yet," I answered; "I have one or two things to do first."

I really had one or two things to do; but it was not so much on that account that I allowed him to drive away alone as because I knew, by a sort of intuition, that Mr Gascoigne wanted to speak to me. So strong was that impression on my part that as soon as I was left upon the pavement with the recently-elected M.P., I said somewhat abruptly—

"Well, what is it?"

He smiled, and remarked—

"You are really very quick, Mr Martyn. Yes, it is quite true that I am glad to have this opportunity of saying a few words to you about Arthur. It would be idle to blink the fact that he and I are, simply and solely through his choice, in the position of antago-nists, and I daresay I may assume that you are on his side in an antagonism which I am un-aware of having done anything to provoke. It is just because you are on his side, because you are a friend of his, and because you are be-

lieved to have influence over him, that I am
anxious to convey a hint to him, through you,
to which he certainly would not listen if it were
to come directly from me. I am not, believe
me, malicious. I have no desire to injure him;
but I believe that I have it in my power to injure him somewhat seriously, and circumstances
may arise which will leave me no option but
to exercise that power. To speak quite candidly, I allude to his attentions to Miss St
George. For reasons upon which I need not
enter, those attentions are as disagreeable to
me as they are to the young lady's aunt, and
they really must be discontinued. If they are
not, I fear that I shall be driven, much against
my will, to have recourse to the measures at
which I have hinted."

"I don't call that speaking quite candidly,"
I replied. "One would like to have something
more definite than a hint before taking upon
oneself to meddle with other people's affairs."

"Quite so, but it will be obvious to you that
I cannot be more explicit without betraying
what I trust may remain a family secret.

Arthur, I have no doubt, has told you of a conversation which I had with him at Lavenham. I must leave you to draw your own conclusions as to the nature of the secret in question."

"I understand then," said I, "that your threat is this. Your cousin is to stop flirting with Miss St George, or else you will circulate some scandalous story, true or false, about his father, and although you failed to frighten him by that threat, you think I may do so. I am obliged to you for your considerate suggestion, but I am not going to take advantage of it, and I will tell you why. I don't believe you can prove anything. Had you been able to do so, you would have come forward with your proofs long before this."

"Do you imagine, Mr Martyn," asked Mr Gascoigne, gravely, "that the credit of the family name counts for nothing with me?"

"It can't count for much," I rejoined, "since you propose to sacrifice it, unless you are gratified by a surrender which certainly will not be made. I couldn't ask Hurstbourne to make that surrender, even if I believed in your power to throw discredit upon anybody except yourself; but I don't. Good morning."

I marched off with my head in the air and with perfect consciousness of having made a foe. It did not, however, seem likely that Mr Gascoigne would ever be able to do me much harm, while he would assuredly do Hurstbourne all the harm he could, whether his conditions were complied with or not. Therefore I did not think that I had been guilty of a diplomatic error by dealing with him in that high and mighty fashion, nor did I deem it advisable to report a menace to which I was disposed to attach very little importance.

Both Hurstbourne and Lady Charles were dining out that evening, and had, I believe, other engagements as well, so that I did not go with them to Lady Deverell's ball. It was close upon midnight when I arrived in Upper Grosvenor Street, for I had not hurried myself, knowing that my personal participation in the revels would be of that passive kind which soon palls upon the participator. The street

was blocked with carriages and the house with
guests, insomuch that it took me a good ten
minutes to reach the landing at the top of the
stairs, the nose of my hostess—*late refulgens*—
serving me as a beacon towards which to shape
my course. I gathered that she must have
been blowing it more than usual, and consequently that she must be more than usually
out of temper—which, indeed, I found to be
the case as soon as I joined her.

"Oh, how do you do?" she said, in an acri-
monious tone. "Your sister has been inquiring
for you; she thought you weren't coming. The
Duke of Hurstbourne has been here for ever so
long. He seems bent upon making a night
of it."

I edged my way on towards the ball-room
without stopping to ask her to explain herself.
I know what women are when their tempers
have been upset; they are just like certain
breeds of dogs, who, the moment that they become excited, must needs bite somebody and
would as soon bite their best friends as anybody else. Hurstbourne, I presumed from Lady

Deverell's remarks, was making fierce love to Miss St George somewhere or other; but I really couldn't help it if he was. The utmost that I could do was to see for myself what he was about, and then endeavour to restrain the noble ire of Mr Paul Gascoigne, supposing that gentleman to be present. However, it was some little time before I could see anything except the backs and heads of persons immediately in front of me. It was all very well for Lady Charles Gascoigne to assert that Lady Deverell knew nobody, and possibly she did not know the smartest of the smart, but she had contrived to get together an enormous number of people, amongst whom I recognised (from having had the privilege of gazing at their photographs in the shop windows) quite a respectable sprinkling of notabilities. Her ball was very well done, too; the flowers alone must have cost her as much money as would have provided me with the necessaries of life for six months.

While I was making my little observations the music ceased, and presently Nora, in the

wake of other couples, passed close beside me.
She at once disengaged herself from the arm
of her cavalier to take possession of mine,
whispering—

"Let us get out of this for a minute, Phil; I
want to speak to you."

After we had extricated ourselves with a
struggle from the surging throng, I led her, or
rather she led me, to the extreme top of the
staircase, where we seated ourselves upon the
floor in accordance with what, I am given to
understand, is the custom, and having indeed
nothing else to sit upon.

"Well," she began, somewhat impatiently,
"have you done anything?"

"Done anything?" I repeated. "No; I
haven't done anything particular that I am
aware of. I haven't warned Hurstbourne off
from the neighbourhood of Miss St George, if
that is what you mean. I don't much believe
in the danger, but if I did believe in it, the
very last thing that I should do would be to
wave a danger flag before his eyes."

"The danger is real, Phil, whether you be-

lieve in it or not. He has been dancing with
her the whole evening. I don't exactly know
what you mean by waving danger flags, but I
should have told him what you and I overheard the other day. That, surely, would have
opened his eyes."

"To what, my dear? To the agreeable circumstances that Lady Deverell and Miss St
George had noticed the very thing that he
was anxious to force upon their notice, and
that you had played the part which he was
graciously pleased to assign to you to per-
fection."

"No; only, perhaps, to the fact that he has
treated me as no gentleman ought to treat a
friend."

"Ah, that is another matter," I said. "If
you wanted me to mention that to him, you
should have said so; and I'm not sure that
I shouldn't have obeyed your instructions.
But I understood that you regarded him and
his flirtations with absolute indifference."

"That only means that you are vexed with
me, as well as with him, and that you won't

stir a finger to help either of us. I thought you were a better friend than that, Phil."

"I am a friend like another," I replied crossly (for, I suppose, the truth was that she had drawn a fairly accurate sketch of my mental condition); "only it seems to me that friendship implies some sort of reciprocity. I have told Hurstbourne over and over again that he will be an ass to propose to Miss St George; what more can I do? If you think I should prove my friendship for you or for him by telling him that, in your opinion and mine, he has behaved very like a cad to you, I am willing to go that length. It will be a little bit humiliating to have to do it, though."

"I daresay it would — and I daresay it wouldn't answer our purpose either," agreed Nora, getting up. "All I know is that I, personally, have submitted to as much humiliation as I can bear. He has reached the end of my patience. I shouldn't so much have minded his dancing with me and sitting out dances with me and all that, if he hadn't thought it necessary to play the whole comedy. It wasn't necessary. He might just as well have talked about hunting, or about anything else that would have given us the appearance of being deeply interested in one another; but, instead of that, he must needs say things which— Well, I'm not going to let him speak to me again as he spoke this evening—even to keep him out of the reach of Miss St George's clutches."

This was pleasant hearing for an already irate brother. I was about to demand a fuller explanation when Hurstbourne himself ran breathlessly up the last flight of stairs to join us.

"So there you are, Miss Nora!" he exclaimed. "I hope you feel ashamed of yourself. You can't have forgotten that you promised me the dance which is just over."

"Is it over?" she returned. "Then I may as well sit down again." And she suited the action to the word. "Phil and I are enjoying ourselves together," she added. "We mustn't keep you in this remote spot, or you won't be able to find your partner for the next dance."

He stared at her with a comical mixture of surprise and penitence.

"What have I done?" he asked. "Why am I to be first thrown over and then kicked downstairs?"

One often laughs when one is not feeling particularly merry. His phrase brought to my memory a familiar quotation, the first words of which struck me as so painfully, ridiculously appropriate that I burst into one of those abrupt guffaws for which I have all my life enjoyed an unenviable celebrity.

By the time that I had composed myself Hurstbourne was half-way down towards the landing, looking extremely huffy, while Nora's pale cheeks were suffused with the rosy hue of wrath. The uproar of my own hilarity had prevented me from hearing what passed between them; but no doubt she had given him the recollection of a waspish speech to take away with him.

She left my side almost immediately afterwards—a partner having come up to claim her; and, during the rest of the evening I saw her only from a distance.

From a distance also I surveyed the other actors in the little drama with which I was concerned — Miss St George, who looked superbly handsome and triumphant; Hurstbourne, who seemed to be in one of his reckless moods; and the future Chancellor of the Duchy of Lancaster, at whose elbow black Care had evidently stationed herself. By watching the pantomime which unfolded itself at intervals before me, I could form a pretty shrewd conjecture at what they were all doing and saying. Sometimes they were together; sometimes one of them—Paul Gascoigne—was left out in the cold. Once, I fancied that there was a sort of incipient altercation between him and Hurstbourne; but it came to nothing, and shortly after two o'clock the politician went away—beaten out of the field, I assumed.

I hardly know why I myself lingered on

until sunrise. Perhaps I wanted to walk home
with Hurstbourne (Lady Charles had long
since departed) and to hear the worst from
his lips. Anyhow, I did wait for him; and
one result of my having done so was that I
was present when he at last took leave of
his hostess. He congratulated her upon the
success of her ball and said it had been
"awfully jolly."

"I am glad you have enjoyed yourself," she
returned, glaring at him, "because you will
never enjoy yourself in this house again; nor
will you ever dance with Leila again. I
cautioned you at supper-time that I wouldn't
have it, but, for reasons best known to yourself, you have chosen to defy me. So much
the worse for you. You don't understand;
but you will before this time to-morrow.
Don't blame me, that's all; I gave you fair
warning, remember."

"What can she have meant?" I asked
Hurstbourne, as we left the house.

"I really don't know, and I really don't
care," he said, laughing and lighting a cigar;

"I suppose she meant that she was in a devil of a rage."

After all, I might as well have gone to bed some hours earlier, for he gave me no chance of interrogating him. He belonged to one of those clubs which are kept open all night, and thither he now saw fit to betake himself, remarking that it was too late, or too early, for respectable people to be seen entering their homes. Probably, he did not wish to be interrogated.

CHAPTER VIII.

ASSAULT AND BATTERY.

ONE does not pretend — at least, I don't pretend—to solve all the enigmas which are for ever cropping up before one as one wends one's straightforward way through the intricacies of a complicated world. Some of them are not worth solving; others demand a sacrifice of time and ingenuity which cannot be bestowed upon them. All things considered, it is best, as a general rule, to wait for the development of events. So, although I do not deny that my curiosity had been stimulated by several of the episodes which had marked Lady Deverell's ball, I made no effort to allay it, knowing very well that I should hear all I wanted to hear before I was much older.

As a matter of fact, I had to wait no longer

than until the ensuing afternoon, when Hurstbourne entered my little writing-room, carrying
a letter in his hand which he said he wished
me to read.

"It was brought to me half an hour ago," he
explained. "I shouldn't wonder if the whole
thing was an infernal lie; but, whether it's a
lie or whether it's true, it must be looked into.
Just read what the fellow says and give me
your opinion about it, will you?"

"The fellow, I presume," said I, as I took
the document handed to me, "is Mr Gascoigne."

Hurstbourne nodded. He looked very savage
and very cool. He is one of those favoured
mortals who grow cool when they are really
angry.

"I won't express my opinion or my intentions yet," he remarked. "Read his letter,
and judge for yourself what you would do in
my place."

The letter, which bore signs of being a pains-
taking composition, ran as follows:—

"MY DEAR COUSIN,—It would, I fear, be

an almost hopeless task to convince you that, in adopting the course which I feel constrained to adopt, I am actuated by no sentiments of personal unfriendliness towards you. You have persistently, though erroneously, credited me with such sentiments, and I am not sanguine enough to expect that this communication will be attributed by you to any other motive. Nevertheless, you will probably understand that I should not, if I could see my way to avoid it, act in such a manner as to cast a slur upon the family to which we both belong. Having premised that much, I will state my case in as few words as possible.

"You have not, I am sure, forgotten a conversation which took place between us at Lavenham upon the subject of the late Lord Charles Gascoigne. Like the rest of the world, you must have surmised that my uncle would not for so many years have refused to recognise his brother without good and sufficient reasons, and that those reasons, if divulged, would in all likelihood prove less creditable to Lord Charles than to the Duke. From information

which had come to my ears at the time,
I was inclined to take that view; but I was
not then, as I am now, in possession of
irrefragable proofs wherewith to support it.
Consequently, when you assumed an indignant
attitude (for which, I assure you, I did not
hold you in the least to blame), I felt that I
was in honour bound to withdraw what you
stigmatised as offensive insinuations. I am
otherwise situated to-day, since I have before
me a document, written and signed by my
late Uncle Charles, which places my suspicions
beyond all reach of contradiction. I am unwilling to cause you any unnecessary pain;
still, when a fact has to be stated, it is perhaps
less cruel to state it without ambiguity than
to beat about the bush. In plain words, then,
your father was a forger. He forged his
brother's name to a cheque for a considerable
amount; he was detected, and he was pardoned.
That is to say that the Duke pardoned him
in so far as to pay the money and to make
him an annual allowance until his marriage
with a lady of large private means rendered

an allowance superfluous. He declined, however, to see or speak to him again; and, as
you are aware, he did not choose to run the
risk of nominating a forger's son as his heir.
The late Duke was a singularly just and clear-
headed man. He was also, in my poor judgment, singularly generous. The promise of
secrecy which he gave to his brother was
never violated by him, I am persuaded, either
in word or by implication.

"You may ask why, under these circumstances,
I should write to you with the evident idea of
breaking an engagement which I may be said
to have in some sort inherited. The question
is a reasonable one, and I will at once give my
answer, although you will probably have anticipated it. Certainly I do not wish the world
to be informed that an uncle of mine was an
unconvicted felon, and certainly I shall with-
hold that information, if it be in my power to
do so. But I have not only myself to consider
in this matter. Without going into motives, to
which, I fear, you would attach scant credence,
I am, I think, entitled at least to say that a

lady for whom I entertain a high regard must not be permitted to accept in ignorance the hand of a man of your parentage. Such, at any rate, is the light in which my duty presents itself to me. Desist from your attentions to Miss St George, and your secret shall be safe; continue them, and I shall be compelled to speak out. Believe me, I sympathise with you in your dilemma, which has not been of my creating; but, pray, believe me also when I assure you that my determination is unalterable.

"I have only to add that, should you be disinclined to accept my word for the facts, I will willingly show you the letter to which I have referred, and that I shall remain at home during the whole of this afternoon, in case of your desiring to see me. I am, my dear Cousin, very faithfully yours,

"PAUL GASCOIGNE."

"Well," said Hurstbourne, when I folded up this gracefully-worded epistle and restored it to him, "what do you think of that?"

"What could anybody think?" I returned sorrowfully. "The man must have his proofs, or he would never have dared to write in that way. I don't know why the sins of the fathers should be visited upon the children; it seems to me a most unjust and abominable law; but I suppose it is one of the laws by which the course of this world has always been governed. You will have to give in, my poor fellow. After all, I can't bring myself to call the terms of surrender hard, and depend upon it, you won't call them so a short time hence."

But Hurstbourne, as I might have known, was not the man to surrender upon any terms, hard or easy, so long as he had a kick left in him.

"We'll see about giving in when we are beaten," he remarked with a grim look about the corners of his mouth. "I can't tell at present whether Paul Gascoigne is a liar or only a cowardly sneak; but I'll find out presently. I'm going round to his house, and you'll have to come with me, Martyn."

"I don't see in what way my presence is likely to be of use," I answered. "If the family dirty linen is to be washed, it had better be washed in private, and I'm afraid I shouldn't act as a restraining force upon Mr Gascoigne, supposing that he has made up his mind to go in for a public display."

Hurstbourne said that wasn't the question. Of course, no representations on my part, or on the part of any other man who had the feelings of a gentleman, would avail to shake the purpose of that self-satisfied cad; but there were occasions on which it was as well to be provided with a witness.

"Besides," he added, "I may want you. I shouldn't wonder if there was going to be a row, and in a row a long-armed, muscular chap like you is pretty apt to be valuable."

This was indeed a pleasing prospect! Was I to be asked to knock Mr Paul Gascoigne M.P., down and sit on his head while Hurstbourne rifled his pockets? Anyhow, I thought I had better accompany him, not as an aggressor but as a peacemaker, and accordingly I made no further protest.

The doors of the spacious mansion in Park Lane which had served several successive Dukes of Hurstbourne as a London residence, and where Paul Gascoigne now dwelt all by himself, were thrown open to receive us, and we were conducted across a waste of faded Turkey carpet to a somewhat sombre study, in which the eminent legislator was discovered 'seated at his writing-table and apparently immersed in correspondence. He rose and held out his hand to Hurstbourne, (who did not seem to notice it), while he honoured me with a bow of faintly surprised recognition.

"I suppose, Arthur," he began mellifluously, "you have come in consequence of my letter? I think it was quite wise of you to come and I am glad you have done so; but— wouldn't it be almost better for us to have our little talk without an audience?"

"Mr Martyn," replied Hurstbourne, "has seen your letter and knows all about it.

For reasons of my own, I preferred to bring him with me, and anything that you have to say may just as well be said before him as not."

"Pray, please yourself," returned Mr Gascoigne, in the same suave accents; "it was on your account, not on my own, that I objected, and I have no doubt that you are justified in placing implicit reliance upon Mr Martyn's discretion. Since he has seen my letter, it is unnecessary for me to acquaint him with the very painful and—er—shameful event about which I had to write to you, and I daresay I may assume that you and he have called in order to satisfy yourselves that I possess documentary proofs of the truth of my statement."

Hurstbourne said—"Exactly so. Now, produce your documentary proof, please."

"I hold it in my hand," answered Mr Gascoigne, opening a drawer and taking out a folded sheet of notepaper; "but before submitting it to your inspection it would be as well, for the sake of lucidity, that I should inform you of certain episodes connected with your father's early life."

Hurstbourne, I am sorry to say, forgot himself so far as to exclaim—

"Damn your lucidity and your episodes, too! Give me that paper and have done with it."

He looked so pugnacious that Mr Gascoigne glanced apprehensively at the bell, and I judged it appropriate to intervene.

"By all means let us have the episodes," said I; "only I am sure you will understand, Mr Gascoigne, that your cousin is naturally impatient to arrive at results and that the less time we waste upon prefatory observations the better."

"I will be brief then," our tormentor rejoined, with an unfriendly side-glance at me. "If I am also compelled to appear curt and unfeeling, the fault will not be mine. From information which I have received, I gather that my unfortunate uncle, the late Lord Charles Gascoigne, went astray at the very outset of his career. He took to betting

and racing, as — as others have done, and,
it would seem, with as little experience or
knowledge to guide him as others have been
equipped with. The usual consequences en-
sued; he became involved in difficulties out
of which his brother, the late Duke, helped
him repeatedly; he had recourse—so at least
I am led to infer—to various more or less
discreditable expedients for raising the wind;
finally, in what I can only regard as an
access of temporary insanity, he actually went
the length of forging the Duke's name to
a cheque. Detection was certain to follow
and did follow, with the result that you
know of. All this, or the essential part of
it, you have already heard; but to enable
you to understand the letter which I shall
presently show you, I must mention that
there was just one redeeming point in an
otherwise — h'm — worthless character. Lord
Charles was, or at any rate pretended to be,
devotedly attached to Miss Julia Nesfield, a
lady who was at that time young and—er
—no doubt beautiful, and with whom you are

well acquainted under her present name of Lady Deverell."

I could not help ejaculating—"Oh, that's it, is it! I see."

"If you mean, sir," returned the narrator, looking severely at me, "that you see why Lady Deverell would incur any sacrifice rather than permit her niece to marry the son of such a man as the late Lord Charles Gascoigne, I can only applaud your perspicacity, although I hardly see by what means you have arrived at a perfectly just conclusion."

You cannot keep so sententious a donkey as that out of office. I would defy any ministry, no matter how powerful, to do it, backed as he is by his position and his riches.

"I was about to say," he resumed, "when Mr Martyn interrupted me, that Miss Nesfield remained faithful to her unworthy admirer, notwithstanding the opposition of her family and the constant scandals to which his conduct gave rise. At the time when

the forgery was committed he was apparently
upon terms of the most unrestricted intimacy
with her, and then it was that he wrote
the letter which she has now—very rightly
and properly, as I think — handed over to
me, after having kept the disgraceful secret
for so many years. It contains, you will see,
a full admission of his guilt. I am authorised
by Lady Deverell to say that it is only with
extreme reluctance, and under pressure of what
she feels to be a paramount necessity, that
she has at length betrayed him; although he
was not long in betraying her. Upon the
mercenary motives which led him to desert
her in favour of a wealthy heiress it is needless for me to dwell; I have, I hope, said
enough to convince you that respect for his
memory will scarcely deter either Lady
Deverell or me from making use of the
weapon that we possess, should we be
forced to do so. But I trust that we shall
not be so forced. Now you can both of you
read the letter, if you wish."

Hurstbourne snatched it up and ran his eye

over it hastily. I did not look at·it myself; but he afterwards gave me a succinct report of what had been revealed to him through the medium of that faded ink and discoloured paper. The missive, which was addressed to the writer's "Dearest Julia," was full of protestations of eternal love, of profound penitence, of determination to eschew evil and do good for the future — a melancholy and ironical record of broken vows and ephemeral repentance which ought never to have been perused by any human being, save the one to whom it had been so imprudently despatched all those years ago. As a confession, and as evidence of guilt, it was absolute and complete, Hurstbourne said. He added that, such being the case, he could not, of course, suffer it to remain in existence. That, indeed, was what he openly and unhesitatingly announced at the time; whereupon Mr Gascoigne, by a sudden deft movement, and with much presence of mind, repossessed himself of the incriminating document.

Immediately afterwards there was a scuffle.

I can truthfully and honestly say that I don't know how or when I was drawn into it, nor what precise object I had in view, beyond the laudable and respectable one of keeping the peace; but the worst of taking part in scuffles is that one can never tell in what position one may find oneself at the end of them, and, at the risk of forfeiting the reader's esteem, I must confess that, when that one ended, I found myself holding Mr Gascoigne's arms tightly behind his back. He was much excited, he was struggling violently, and he was making use of language which, I am assured, is never heard within the precincts of St Stephen's. Meanwhile, Hurstbourne was deliberately tearing that antediluvian love-letter into little bits and thrusting the fragments into his pocket. A more high-handed and outrageous proceeding I never heard of, and although, as regards the share that I had in it, I might perhaps plead extenuating circumstances, I will not do so. Amongst other compliments which Mr Gascoigne addressed to me in the heat of the moment, he called me a hired bully; it is not for me to deny that he was justified in thus describing me.

However, the letter had now been torn to pieces and could not be put together again (for I was sure Hurstbourne would swallow the scraps rather than allow that experiment to be tried); so that the only question for reasonable men to consider was what was to be done next. Mr Gascoigne wanted to send for the police, but by dint of physical and moral suasion I induced him to relinquish so hasty and ill-advised a plan. I pointed out to him that the evidence upon which he had relied no longer existed, that if he were to give his cousin and me into custody upon a charge of having assaulted and robbed him, he would have extreme difficulty in substantiating his accusation, and that he would assuredly be compelled to reveal certain things over which it would be infinitely better, in the interests of everybody concerned, to draw a veil.

"Admitting," I continued, "that you have some ground for complaint of the manner in

which you have been dealt with, the fact
still remains that you did your best to in-
timidate us. And no man who is worth his salt
will submit to intimidation. Now won't you
sit down and talk matters over quietly and
dispassionately, like a sensible being? It
doesn't seem to me at all impossible that some
compromise may be agreed upon."

After some further parley, he grew calmer
and admitted that, since we had taken care to
be two to one, we were for the time being in
a position to dictate our own terms. He must,
however, reserve complete liberty of future
action to himself. If we spoke of compromise,
all he could say was that the cowardly and
dishonourable act which had just been perpe-
trated would certainly not induce him to consent to any compromise which should include
the possibility of a marriage between Miss St
George and one of his assailants.

"I made the mistake," he remarked, "of supposing that I had to do with gentlemen; you
have chosen to take what I should have imagined to be an impossibly base advantage of

my error. Well and good; but you cannot
close my lips, and I believe that, among gentlemen, my account of this *fracas* will be accepted
rather than yours."

"I think, you know," said I to Hurstbourne,
" that that can't be called an unfair way of putting the case. Mr Gascoigne had no business
to hold a pistol to your head; but you had no
business to ask leave to examine his weapon
and then destroy it. You have both been in
the wrong: can't you both contrive to put
yourselves in the right again by a compact
which will injure neither of you? I do not
understand Mr Gascoigne to say that he himself contemplates marrying Miss St George, but
only that his regard for her will not permit
him to let her marry you. Why, then, should
it not be agreed that, so far as you and he are
concerned, Miss St George shall remain a
spinster? It seems to me—"

"My good Martyn," interrupted Hurstbourne
impatiently, "you mean well, but you talk great
nonsense. I'll fight fairly with any man who
offers to fight me fairly, but when he tries to

stab me in the back I'll beat him the best way
I can. I don't care two straws whether this
fellow calls me dishonourable or not; let him
summons me or take any other measure that
he likes; it's all one to me. Now I have done
what I came here to do, and I'm going away."

Paul Gascoigne made no attempt to inter-
cept him as he moved towards the door, but
merely remarked: "You won't carry your point.
You have forfeited all claim to indulgence from
me, and even if I were disposed to let you
escape scot-free, Lady Deverell would not spare
you. You may take my word for it that she
will not consent to an alliance between you
and her niece."

"That," returned Hurstbourne, "is a question
which may have to be fought out between
Lady Deverell and her niece, or between Lady
Deverell and me; you have nothing to do with
it. What has happened to you is that you
have tried to play me a dirty trick and failed."

I believe Mr Gascoigne expressed his opinion
of us in well-chosen, trenchant terms, but he
offered no opposition to our exit, nor did I listen

very attentively of his parting observations. As soon as we were out in the street I began to scold Hurstbourne roundly, and he paid about as much attention to me as I had paid to his partially-vanquished rival.

"It's all quite true, you know," he said, breaking in abruptly upon my harangue, after we had walked some little distance; "the thing did actually happen just as that brute declared."

"Well, I'm afraid so," I replied, "and that's just the awkward part of it. When you are charged with having done this, that, the other *et cetera*, what line of defence do you propose to adopt, may I ask?"

He did not respond, but presently inquired whether I thought that any girl who respected herself would consent to marry the son of a forger.

"I can't answer for girls," said I. "Individually I should not be so unjust as to hold a son responsible for his father's misdeeds, but women don't so much as know what justice means. I should think she would refuse you.

I quite hope she will, because, in any event, she is one of those expensive luxuries which you can't by any possibility afford."

I expected him to rise, but he didn't. He had taken me by the arm, and, after a pause, during which I noticed that he was not leading me towards Berkeley Square, I made so bold as to ask whither we were bound now.

"Why, we're going to Lady Deverell's of course," he answered. "You didn't suppose that we had got through the day's work yet, did you?"

CHAPTER IX.

THE BEARDING OF THE LIONESS.

I WAS at a loss to understand what useful purpose could be served by a visit to Lady Deverell,
who, in my humble judgment, was made of
sterner stuff than Paul Gascoigne, and with
whom our interview — supposing that we obtained one — seemed likely to prove even more
unpleasant than that which we had just brought
to a quasi-victorious close; but, as Hurstbourne
evidently meant to have his own way, I held
my peace and hoped that her ladyship would
not be at home.

I was disappointed, however; for, on reaching
Upper Grosvenor Street, we were granted admittance and were shown into the empty drawing-room, where we were kept waiting for five
minutes. My apprehension of distressing possi-
sibilities had led me to inquire softly of the

butler whether the young ladies were at home,
and he had replied that they had gone out in
the carriage, which both relieved my mind and
suggested to me that Lady Deverell might not
have been unprepared for a call from one of
us. During the interval of suspense that I
have mentioned Hurstbourne never opened his
lips. He stood on the middle of the hearth-rug,
with his hands behind his back, looking pale,
resolute and ready to fight any man or woman
in the wide world. Nervous though I was and
anxious to be well out of it, I could not help
wondering, with some pleasurable emotion of
curiosity, what sort of a queer encounter I was
about to witness.

Presently the door was thrown open and the
other party to the combat entered the lists.
Her forbidding countenance wore a somewhat
more than usually hard expression; yet I
divined that she was a little ashamed of herself
and a little sorry for the man upon whose head
she had brought down the consequences of a
forgotten disgrace. She did not offer him her
hand, nor did he make any advance towards

according her that customary form of greeting, but I was permitted to press her long, skinny fingers, while she surveyed me interrogatively, as who should say, "Pray, who asked *you* to put your oar in?"

"You have only yourself to thank," she began, addressing Hurstbourne, without preface or any simulated doubt as to the nature of his errand; "a moment's reflection will show you that it was not much more agreeable to me to hand that letter over to Mr Gascoigne, than it can have been to you to read it. But you left me no choice; you refused to listen to repeated warnings—you *would* have it! After all, now that you know the truth, you will hardly assert that you were entitled to expect much consideration from me."

"You think, perhaps," said Hurstbourne, "that I came here to reproach you. Not at all; I only came in order to make my position and yours clear; as matters stand now, it seems to want a little clearing up. What you imagine to be your position is this, isn't it?—that you possess, or rather that your confederate Paul

Gascoigne possesses, an incriminating letter which you are determined to make public unless I comply with certain conditions. In what sort of way you mean to make it public I don't quite understand. Did you propose to communicate it to a news agency?"

"You know as well as I do," returned Lady Deverell, "that the kind of publication that is required for all intents and purposes doesn't mean publication in the newspapers, though it is likely enough that the story will find its way into some of them. That is if you are foolish enough to defy us. If you comply with our conditions — as of course you must — we shall not trouble you any further."

" Well, I shall not comply with your conditions," said Hurstbourne. "As for the penalty with which you threaten me, there is one trifling obstacle in the way of your carrying it out, namely, that your evidence has been scattered to the four winds. I can speak positively upon that point, because I tore your letter into shreds with my own hands only a short time ago."

"You did that!" exclaimed Lady Deverell, her eyes flashing and her lips quivering; "you were guilty of such vile treachery and dishonesty as that! Ah, I might have known that you were your father's son! How could that man have been fool enough to post the letter to you. I told him not to part with it."

"Oh, you mustn't be angry with him," answered Hurstbourne, coolly; "he took every reasonable precaution. He invited me to inspect the document at his house; he didn't know that I should bring a great big friend with me; still less could he anticipate that we should resort to physical violence. As he himself touchingly remarked, he supposed that he had to do with gentlemen."

Like the majority of her sex, Lady Deverell was puzzled and angered by anything approaching irony. She stared and frowned, and then snorted out, "Oh, you don't even pretend to be a gentleman, then?"

"How should I, my dear lady, when you have taken such pains to demonstrate to me that my father ought by rights to have spent

the best years of his life in a convict prison?
You shouldn't destroy a man's self - respect if
you want to keep him nice and scrupulous.
You will be shocked to hear that I am not in
the very slightest degree ashamed of my conduct. Martyn, as you may see by his face, is
a good deal ashamed of having held your
friend down while I destroyed your valuable
property, but Martyn's father was a respectable
man, I daresay, and he himself is about as
respectable as they make them. Naturally he
blushes, and naturally I don't. At all events
there's an end and a finish to your precious
letter, and now what are you going to do
next?"

"I am surprised at your asking," Lady
Deverell declared; "it stands to reason that I
shall—well, that I shall expose you."

"Does it? I should have thought that you
could hardly expose me without exposing
yourself. The threat of exposure would have
been all very well if it had happened to be
effectual, but the reality—isn't that rather a
different thing? I'm afraid some of your

friends will be disrespectful enough to smile when you unfold your tragic tale, and that others will listen to it with a spice of incredulity. It may be true, they will think, that you were jilted ages ago by a man who knew that you had it in your power to blast his reputation at any moment, but it isn't over and above likely to be true. And then they will begin to wonder why, if you meant to reveal the secret at all, you didn't reveal it a little sooner."

"That will easily be explained. I might have revenged myself upon your father if I had condescended to do so, and if I had thought that a mere desire for revenge could ever be justifiable. It is because I did not think so that I have hitherto spared him and you. But now I have a motive—a very sufficient motive—for speaking out, and you know very little about me if you imagine that my mouth will be closed by any fear of the laughter of my friends."

"You really mean to proclaim your motive then? That is courageous of you, though it can't be called discreet. You are really going to announce from the house-tops that your reason for accusing my father of a crime which can't possibly be proved against him is that you are in terror lest your niece should have bestowed her affections upon my father's son? There is one person who won't thank you for your candour, and that is Miss St George."

"I could have proved him guilty," cried Lady Deverell, a dull red colour coming into her faded cheeks. "I have only been deprived of my proof by your infamous brutality. You don't even affect to deny that, and if you did, I could call Mr Gascoigne, and that foolish young Martyn, whom I am sorry to see in his present disgraceful situation, as witnesses."

"No doubt. Still you would be left in the painful predicament of having placed Miss St George in a predicament even more painful than your own. Your dilemma would have been pretty much the same if I had left Paul Gascoigne in undisturbed possession of your proofs; but he isn't a very trustworthy person, so I thought it as well to be on the safe side."

"In other words, you imagine that after what you have done, you can bully me into silence. You will find that you have made a miscalculation. Up to the present moment I have not said one word to Leila, but this evening she shall hear the whole truth."

"That is of course. Did you think that I wished to conceal it from her? But where will you be if, in spite of having heard the whole truth, she tells you that her affections have been bestowed unworthily?"

"She will not do so. She is a gentlewoman, and it would be impossible for her to feel any affection for a forger's son."

"Oh, I don't know about the impossibility. You were not unwilling, it seems, to marry the forger himself. I don't blame you for that; I can quite forgive you; but will Miss St George forgive your suggesting that she is ready to throw herself into the arms of a humble and disgraced individual who hasn't yet asked her to marry him?"

"That is begging the question. You are going to ask her to marry you."

"Perhaps. Anyhow, I shall do exactly as I feel disposed about it, and I shall not ask your permission. You said a short while ago that I wasn't entitled to expect much consideration from you: now I don't think you are entitled to expect much consideration from me."

"I am not asking you for any," Lady Deverell declared, with some emotion; "yet if you had a spark of honourable or gentlemanly feeling, you would acknowledge that I have not been ungenerous to you and yours. I have kept your shameful secret, and I should have kept it to my dying day but for your impudent attempt to thrust yourself into my family. Oh, I understand your smile; your retort is easy, and you haven't shrunk from making it already. I was willing to marry a forger! Yes, I was willing to marry him, because I cared for him and believed that he cared for me, and because I was too young to know that a man who had done such a thing was certain to do other things as bad and worse. It is worthy of a Gascoigne to sneer at me

for my folly. But now I am older and wiser;
now I am determined to save others from such
a misfortune as nearly overtook me, and it is
not the dread of being laughed at, or even of
being disbelieved, that will deter me from
doing my duty."

I broke silence for the first time to remark,—"That isn't so badly put."

The words were forced from me by my admiration for the genuine excitement which had
momentarily transformed a sour old woman
into a sort of tragedy queen, but the chief
actors I suppose did not feel any need of a
chorus, for neither of them vouchsafed me the
slightest attention. Hurstbourne said gravely—

"Look here, Lady Deverell; you were badly
treated once upon a time, I have no doubt,
and you were entitled to choose your own
opportunity for paying off old scores. I don't
condemn you, but, at the same time, I don't
think it lies in your mouth to condemn me.
It's a case of pot and kettle. To serve my
own selfish ends I haven't scrupled to commit
a species of felony, and to serve your own

selfish ends you haven't scrupled to do things which, in my humble opinion, are just as felonious as if they were punishable by the law of the land. It really isn't worth our while to call each other names."

"I have done nothing felonious and nothing wrong," the old lady returned; "still less have I done anything selfish. It was for my niece's sake, not for my own, that I felt bound to take that letter out of the desk in which I have kept it locked up for more years than you have lived in the world."

"Ah, I wasn't thinking about the letter; I was thinking about your treatment of a girl to whom you were supposed to be acting in the capacity of a mother. It was very pretty and very unselfish on your part to offer hospitality and protection to Miss Martyn, wasn't it? You knew—or at all events, you thought you knew—that I had not the smallest intention of asking her to be my wife; but that was no reason why there shouldn't be a flirtation between us or why the flirtation shouldn't have results which would exactly suit your book. I am not going to tell you how I discovered your amiable little design, but I have discovered it, as you see, and upon my word, I don't see what business you have to mount the high horse when you talk to me. If I am a despicable being, it strikes me very forcibly that you are another."

Lady Deverell was visibly disconcerted. I don't know whether she would have met his assertion with a flat contradiction if she had not been hampered by the memory of a certain conversation which I had overheard, but I daresay she would not, for she had an unusual share of masculine attributes. What she did deny, in a few words, was that she had ever trifled with my sister's happiness.

"Miss Martyn," said she, bluntly and somewhat inelegantly, "wouldn't touch you with a pair of tongs; you may make your mind as easy as mine is on that score. Think just what you please about me; I don't value your good opinion. Am I to understand, then, that you intend to persist in your courtship of Leila St George?"

"I thought I had told you already that I should do exactly as I felt disposed; I only wondered whether you would be foolish enough to go in for public revelations."

"Private revelations will probably suffice," answered Lady Deverell drily; "but, to use your own words, I shall do exactly as I feel disposed."

"I see," observed Hurstbourne. "Then I think we have pretty well exhausted the subject and may wish you good-bye."

We effected our retreat with more or less of ostensible dignity, but I could not feel that we had cut a very dignified figure in the above encounter, and the moment we were once more out in the open air, I endeavoured to show my companion how hopeless was the struggle to which he had committed himself.

"It is possible," I said, "that Lady Deverell and Mr Gascoigne may keep their own counsel, because I don't suppose that they are either of them particularly anxious to provoke the hilarity of their neighbours, but you must indeed be sanguine if you expect Miss St George to accept you after the 'private revelation' which is about to be made to her."

"Who told you that she would get the chance?" asked Hurstbourne tranquilly.

"I was under the impression that you had," I replied.

"You were under a false impression, then. That girl has no more heart than a stone! It was she who enlightened me about your sister and the old woman's designs. She did it at the ball, and I was much obliged to her for opening my eyes. Oh, they're a nice lot, these women!"

"It has always been my conviction that the vices of the sex are in excess of its virtues," I remarked.

"With one exception, eh? Well, I grant you the one exception. Perhaps, if it wasn't asking too much of you, you might consent to throw my mother in, but I won't insist upon it. Poor old mother; this will be a sad blow for her!"

"The discovery that you have lost all esteem for her sex in general and for Miss St George in particular?"

"No; don't laugh—there's nothing to laugh
at. I mean the discovery that we are eternally
disgraced. Perhaps it won't be a discovery,
though—who knows? We shall have to hide our
heads somewhere or other abroad, I suppose.
Well, we should have had to go into exile any-
way, for I'm about broke. All the same, I didn't
make a bad fight for it when I was driven into
the last ditch, did I?"

I could not quite bring myself to commend
his method of fighting; but it seemed rather
absurd to have fought so hard only in order
to run away. I comforted him to the best of
my ability, pointing out that, with a little
courage and a good deal of economy, his affairs
still admitted of re-establishment upon a solid
basis, and recommending him, if he did decide
to leave the country, to do so only by way of
preparing himself and his associates for the
inevitable change which would have to take
place in his manner of living after his return.
As for eternal disgrace, that was nonsense.
Since he really didn't want to marry Miss
St George, he might safely count, I thought,

upon the silence of Lady Deverell and his cousin.

"My dear fellow, they may have the whole story printed in the form of a leaflet and stand at Hyde Park Corner, distributing copies to the passers-by all day long, if they choose," he returned; "the disgrace is in there being such a story to tell, not in its being told."

"Yet, for the sake of destroying the evidence, you have risked getting yourself and me into a horrible mess," I remarked, with a shade of irritation. "Why on earth did you do that?"

"Now that you ask me, I hardly know. I suppose I wanted to show Paul Gascoigne that, if it came to bullying, two could play at that game. Very likely, as you say, he and that old woman will hold their tongues now; but it makes no difference, because I sha'n't be able to hold mine. I mean, I shall always have to confess the truth to anybody whom I — well, to anybody whose opinion signifies. You are good enough to declare that you wouldn't hold a man responsible for his father's misdeeds; but you admitted, when I asked you, that no girl who respected herself could marry a son of a forger."

"I never said that," I replied; "I said I didn't think Miss St George would accept you; but it is no longer a question of Miss St George, thank Heaven! It will be time enough to bother yourself when there comes to be a question of somebody else; but that won't be yet awhile, I hope. The truth is that you are too young and, considering your rank, too poor to think of marrying at present."

"My chances wouldn't be greatly improved if I were older and richer, I expect," he returned despondently. "I wonder whether you would work yourself up into an awful rage if I told you something, Martyn."

I answered that his conduct, for a long time past, had enraged me to that extent that it would be difficult to conceive of any confession which could enrage me further.

"I'm not so sure of that," said Hurstbourne; "still, I should rather like to make a clean breast of it to you. That can't do either you or me any harm, if it doesn't do us any good. I daresay I was mistaken, but I thought perhaps you might have guessed that I had fallen in love with your sister when we were down in the country. I won't deny that I tried to get over it as soon as I found it out; I had an idea that I ought to marry somebody with aristocratic connections if I could, and I did, for a time, think of marrying Miss St George, not because I cared a pin about her, but because I wanted to cut that fellow Paul out. I should never have done it, though. I couldn't have brought myself to the point of proposing to her, even if she hadn't made me hate her by the way in which she spoke about your sister that night at the ball. I knew before then that there was only one person in the world who could ever be my wife, and that person never will be my wife now. It wouldn't be the slightest use to ask her, would it?"

I hesitated for a moment (the complicated aspect of the situation being very apparent to me) before I replied—

"I don't think it would be much use, Hurstbourne. I am sure that if Nora cared for you, she wouldn't be influenced in the smallest degree by anything that you might see fit to tell her about your father's shortcomings, but I doubt very much whether she does care for you. You haven't exhibited yourself in a particularly becoming light to her, you see. Candour deserves to be met with candour, so I'll admit that you might have won her heart at one time if you had tried to do so, but by your own admission, you tried to do the contrary. I should imagine that you have been completely successful. Take my advice, and let the whole affair pass into the category of might-have-beens. The things that might have been wouldn't always have turned out well if they had been, and, after all, we don't belong to the class from which dukes and duchesses are recruited—Nora and I."

I confess that the meekness with which Hurstbourne bowed to my ruling disappointed me a little. I thought that he would have been less submissive if he had been really in earnest, and I didn't quite see why he should have mentioned Nora's name to me at all, unless he had been in earnest. I was, however, convinced that she had overcome her temporary infatuation, and, since that was the case, it was perhaps just as well that she should not be unsettled by an offer which she would have had no choice but to refuse. The remainder of our walk was accomplished in unbroken silence.

CHAPTER X.

FEMININE CONSISTENCY.

IT does not seem impossible that, in the course of the humble narrative which is now nearing its conclusion, I may have conveyed to feminine readers an impression that I am incapable of comprehending or rendering justice to their sex. To that criticism most of them will probably add that they can get on very well without my comprehension or my justice. Perhaps, therefore, it would be impertinent on my part to offer excuses and apologies; still, if I can't do justice to others, I am always anxious to do justice to myself, and that is why I seize this opportunity of declaring how fully I recognise and admire the power of women to come out strong in times of emergency. Personally, I think they would be pleasanter to live with if they did not habitually exaggerate the proportions

177

of molehills by way of offset to their occasional courage in levelling mountains, but this is neither here nor there. I gladly admit that they possess the latter form of courage, and Lady Charles Gascoigne, of all people in the world, gave us a splendid example of it when we informed her that, in consequence of the recent ducal extravagances, the ducal *ménage* would have to be speedily shorn of all its magnificence.

"Oh, well," she said, after I had broken the news to her as considerately as I could, and had spoken of the proposed reductions in her son's establishment as not only commendable but really indispensable, "that isn't so bad, you know; it isn't ruin, and it isn't bankruptcy. We shall go abroad for a year or two and amuse ourselves very well in an economical way until things come round, and I am sure Mr Martyn will do his best for us during our absence. Do you think of letting Hurstbourne, Arthur? There ought to be no trouble about finding a tenant."

Hurstbourne embraced her, swearing that no

man had ever had so good a mother and that few mothers had ever been afflicted with such a fool of a son. I suppose that, in a certain sense, the poor woman had been a good mother to him; at all events she had been a most affectionate one, and I must say that she behaved on this occasion far better than I had dared to anticipate. While they were exchanging endearing epithets and trying to persuade one another that it was really rather fun than otherwise to descend once more into obscurity from those sun-illumined heights upon which their sojourn had been so brief, I slipped out of the room. I knew that there was something else to be said, something which could hardly be made light of and which had better not be alluded to in the presence of a third person; so I escaped to my private den, where I set about making preparations for the winding up and resigning of my stewardship.

I had been wrestling for rather more than half an hour with the intricacies of unmanageable figures when a tremulous tap at the door the heralded entrance of Lady Charles. I had felt quite sure that she would seek me out, and had hoped against hope that she wouldn't. What, indeed, could I say to her, and what possible comfort was it in my power to offer her? I did my best, and she seemed relieved to hear that, in my opinion, there was little or no likelihood of the history of her late husband's misdemeanours being made public property; but of course I could not tell her that I thought that defunct scamp justified in having signed another man's name, and, upon my honour, I believe that was what she wanted me to say. It was so terrible, she moaned, after she had cast herself down upon a chair and had allowed her tears to run unrestrainedly down her poor old painted cheeks, that Arthur should be driven to despise his father. Well, it was terrible, no doubt, only I did not see how Arthur was to help it, and I remarked that he had at least done what in him lay to protect his father's memory.

"Oh, yes," she sobbed, "he has acted nobly and generously, and like his father's son!" A comic and pathetic tribute of applause to our joint exploit. "And I am very grateful to you," she added, "for having helped him to silence that cold-blooded villain. You have shown yourself a true friend to Arthur, Mr Martyn; I shall never forget it."

"Thank you," I answered, "but we are not out of the wood yet, and I am by no means sure that we haven't done a stupid day's work between us. Our chief hope of escaping the penalty due to our offence is that your son apparently no longer wishes to promote Miss St George to the highest rank in the peerage. Did he tell you that?"

"Yes," she answered, "he told me that, and —and other things besides. I was very glad —and very sorry. I mean, I was glad that he has no real affection for that girl; because she isn't a nice girl. Paul Gascoigne may take her if he can get her, and I wish him joy of his bargain. It isn't that sort of thing that signifies."

What, according to her, did signify was the pessimistic view which Hurstbourne had taken up of a bygone and condoned offence. I agreed

with her that no shadow of blame rested upon
him, but I could not quite follow her in her
elaborate attempt to prove that the late Lord
Charles Gascoigne had not been so very much
to blame either. She had a good deal to say
upon the subject; she made out as good a case
for her husband as could have been made out;
it is likely enough that her husband would
have resisted temptation as successfully as the
rest of us, if only he had not happened to find
temptation irresistible. The touching part of
her incoherent narrative consisted in the un-
conscious evidence of her own absolute un-
selfishness, which she displayed in every sentence
of it. She had married a more or less penitent
scapegrace, whom she had adored and who had
perhaps been fond of her after a fashion which
had not deterred him from squandering her
fortune; when he had been taken from her, she
had devoted herself, heart and soul, to her son,
for whose sake she had cheerfully submitted to
a thousand discomforts and petty miseries; the
only thing that rendered her disconsolate now
was that, notwithstanding all her precautions,

her son had at length been let into a secret which, she sadly feared, had broken his heart.

I endeavoured to reassure her. Naturally, she did not attach much importance to my assertion that hearts are not broken so easily as all that; but she appeared to be in some measure consoled by the convincing terms in which I represented to her that, from the moment their quarry was released, neither Lady Deverell nor Mr Gascoigne could have any conceivable motive for disclosing what she was so eager to bury in oblivion. She left the room at last in a somewhat happier frame of mind, and, I daresay, went upstairs to conceal the traces of her emotion beneath the customary coat of rouge and whitewash. I was thankful to her for her delicacy in abstaining from any reference to Nora (because it was evident that Hurstbourne had been as frank with her as he had been with me), and also for the matter-of-course way in which she received the announcement of my impending resignation. I had been prepared for some useless opposition and remonstrance on the latter head.

I did subsequently meet with some opposition from Hurstbourne, who seemed to think that he had involved me in his downfall and who reproached himself for having caused me, as he phrased it, to "make a false start" in life. He declared that he could see no earthly reason why I should not continue to draw my salary and manage his affairs for him during his absence; he would not accept as a serious excuse (indeed, it was not a very good one) my allegation that he would soon have no affairs to manage; he even went so far as to accuse me of ratting from a sinking ship. However, he had no answer to make when I asked him whether, after the confession that I had had from him, he thought it would be desirable or possible for my sister to live with me while I was living upon his estate. My sister, I added, would have to live with me, because there was nowhere else for her to live. The poor fellow was very meek and submissive. Lady Deverell and Mr Gascoigne would hardly have recognised their brazen-faced assailant in the dejected young man who assured me that nothing except his duty to his mother restrained

him from putting an end to a useless and value-
less existence.

"You will be as valuable as ever in a few
years, if only you will keep very quiet during
that time," I returned, "and you may depend
upon it that plenty of uses will be found for you
before you die. Meanwhile, it would be an
exceedingly cowardly act on your part to hang
yourself, leaving me to be summoned by your
cousin and punished with the utmost vigour of
the law."

But Mr Gascoigne did not take out a summons.
We heard nothing of or from him in the course
of the following day, nor did any communication reach us from Lady Deverell. I took it
that they were waiting for Hurstbourne to make
the next move.

"They'll have to wait a long time, then," he
remarked, on my imparting this view to him.
"I don't know what more there is for me to say
or do. I shouldn't wonder if I were to meet the
old woman to-night, though. I shall be curious
to see whether she will cut me dead or denounce
me publicly."

He was, as usual, dining out and was going on afterwards to I forget whose reception—a huge quasi-political gathering at which Lady Deverell was pretty sure to be present. I did not think it at all probable that she would denounce him; but I was, I confess, not less curious than he as to the reception which her ladyship might see fit to accord to him and a good deal more so, perhaps, as to the method by which Miss St George might contrive to extricate herself from a somewhat puzzling position. Consequently I busied myself with accounts of past expenditure and schemes for future retrenchment until long after midnight, when my patience was rewarded by the entrance of my noble employer, who cast himself down upon a chair and said—

"Throw me a cigar and give me something to drink, will you, like a good chap? Well, I've had a rare evening of it! Everybody has heard that I'm broke, you know."

"Everybody," I remarked, "always does hear of things that haven't yet happened; that's not a matter of much consequence, is it? But I hope everybody hasn't heard of what actually did happen yesterday."

"Not that I'm aware of," he answered, after swallowing the half of the whisky-and-soda which I had poured out for him. "Miss St George has, because she has received full and particular information from her dear old aunt; but she isn't going to talk about it. She said it wouldn't be worth her while, and I quite agreed with her."

"Oh, you saw Miss St George, then?"

"Rather! She doesn't mind calling a spade a spade, that young woman. She led me off into a corner to tell me that she knew the worst and that, upon the whole, she rather admired my pluck or my impudence—she didn't quite know what to call it."

"Well?" I said, after waiting some little time for him to continue.

"Well, we had a longish talk, and I mentioned that I was going to put everything down and leave the country and so forth. Of course I understood what she was driving at, and that she wanted me to give her the satisfaction of having refused me; but, as I declined to come up to the scratch, she ended by asking me point-blank whether I hadn't something to say to her."

"How charmingly ingenuous! And you replied?"

"I replied that I didn't see what there was to be said, except good-bye. Then I don't exactly remember what took place, or how it was that she arrived at the point of calling me every bad name that she could lay her tongue to. I hooked it as soon as I could. The fact is, my dear Martyn," continued Hurstbourne, with the air of one who, by dint of long experience and observation, has discovered a recondite truth, "that an angry woman is the deuce and all! It's no use reasoning with her; it's no use pointing out to her that she hasn't the slightest excuse for being angry with you; the only plan is to bolt. Hang it all! you're not bound to propose to a woman whom you would rather die than marry merely in order that she may boast afterwards of having dismissed you with a flea in your ear."

That proposition was indisputable, and I did not dispute it, although it occurred to me that Miss St George might have more substantial grounds for indignation than the one mentioned. Frankly speaking, it was little enough that I cared about any disappointment which might have been inflicted upon Miss St George and little credit that I gave her for a genuine desire to participate in the self-denials of an exile. I was rejoiced to think that that chapter was closed, and rejoiced also to notice that Hurstbourne's spirits had been to some extent improved by the events of the evening. I am sure he did not suspect at the time, and I doubt whether he has ever suspected since, that he had inspired Lady Deverell's niece with a passion which, by reason of the poverty of language, must be classed under the generic heading of love.

On the succeeding afternoon I was meditating a visit to Upper Grosvenor Street, for the purpose of conferring with Nora and making arrangements for her speedy removal to some place of shelter which I could call my own, when I was spared the trouble of rising from my chair by the arrival of my sister, who, before I could say a word, informed me that she meant to quit Lady Deverell's house on the morrow. She had, it appeared, been made acquainted with the various espisodes of the previous forty-eight hours; so that she was prepared to take up her abode with me provisionally as soon as I should have laid down my present functions.

"Only," said she, "you won't of course be able to leave the Duke for some weeks to come, and I really can't live any longer in the same house with Miss St George. I am sorry to make a fuss; but you would admit that I have no choice in the matter if you had heard the way in which she spoke to me last night. It was at a great crush; the Duke was there, and I suppose he must have given her to understand that he had no intentions. Anyhow, after they had been talking together for some time, she marched up to me in a towering passion and charged me in the plainest of plain terms with having done my utmost to catch him. She didn't mince matters; she said a worm might be a useful bait to attract a fish, but it wasn't the worm who retained possession of him when he had been hooked, and I might take her word for it that, sly as I was, my slyness wouldn't be of any service to me. She was so furious that I daresay she hardly knew what she was saying; but it wasn't particularly pleasant to me to listen to her, and I don't suppose it can have been particularly pleasant to Lady Deverell either. Afterwards Lady Deverell apologised to me and gave me a sort of explanation. She begged me to stay with her as long as I felt inclined, and promised that I shouldn't be so insulted a second time; nevertheless, I don't think she was much grieved to hear that I had already made arrangements for leaving."

"That you had made arrangements?"

"Yes; by a queer stroke of good fortune Uncle John happened to be one of the crowd. I had shaken hands with him a few minutes before; so as soon as Miss St George turned her back upon me, I sought him out and reminded him of an old offer of his. He was quite pleasant about it; he said they would of course be very happy to give me house-room, and he didn't ask more questions than he could help. Naturally, he lamented what he called 'the pecuniary collapse of that foolish young nobleman,' which, he feared, would 'throw Philip out of work again;' but I don't think he suspected the existence of any other intricacies in our relations with the foolish young nobleman. So you see I shall be all right, and you needn't worry yourself about me until you have cleared yourself from more important worries."

I had nothing to urge against an arrangement which, under all the circumstances, seemed to be the wisest and most feasible that could be suggested; but I thought that I ought, perhaps, to say a word or two about Hurstbourne, and I should probably have been clumsy enough to utter those words if Hurstbourne himself had not come into the room before I had quite made up my mind.

On discovering that I was not alone, he

looked slightly taken aback, but at once re-
gained his self-possession, and chattered away
for the next quarter of an hour upon all sorts
of subjects with an assumption of cheerful
carelessness which I could not sufficiently admire. Nora did not behave quite so well.
She was embarrassed, and showed that she
was embarrassed; she answered him at random;
she demonstrated to him as plainly as could
be that she was wondering when he meant
to go away; and, as he displayed no sign of
responding to her tacit invitation, she herself
rose at last, with the somewhat uncivil remark
that we could resume our interrupted colloquy
another day.

"Are you walking home, Miss Martyn?"
asked Hurstbourne, getting up at the same
moment. "I'll walk round with you, if you
don't object, and see you safely over the
crossings."

She did object; but her objections were
disregarded, and her assertion that there are
no crossings worth speaking of between Berkeley Square and Upper Grosvenor Street was

met with a counter-assertion to the effect that
Berkeley Square is just about the most dangerous
place in London to traverse without an efficient
escort. Nobody, so Hurstbourne declared, is
run over in Piccadilly or Cheapside, where there
are refuges and vigilant policemen; but a
tradesman's cart or a hansom cab, rattling
down Hay Hill with a loose rein, is the very
thing of all others most likely to bring about
the death of the unwary pedestrian. They
were still arguing when they departed. Looking out of the window presently, I saw them
walking off, side by side, in the sunshine,
having to all appearance composed or forgotten
their difference. Well, there was perhaps no
great harm, if there was no great good, in
their holding a farewell conversation. In one
sense, the whole thing was a pity; still, the
pity of it might have been even more conspicuous if things had gone moderately straight
with them, instead of immoderately crooked—if
he had not chanced to come across Miss St
George and she had not learnt to appraise
him at a value considerably lower than that

which she had placed upon him in the earlier stages of their intimacy. The old aristocratic notions of what constitutes a *mésalliance*, have, it is true, passed out of date; yet there remains a difference between espousing an American heiress whose relations reside on the other side of the Atlantic and making a duchess out of a British orphan whose father was engaged in commerce and whose commercial undertakings ended disastrously into the bargain. I did not regard it as by any means proved that Nora would have been a happy woman, had the Fates permitted of her becoming Duchess of Hurstbourne.

In some degree soothed by these philosophic cogitations, I returned to my figures; and if ever I was amazed in my life, I was amazed when Hurstbourne burst in upon me towards evening, in a state of insane jubilation, exclaiming—

"It's all right, old man, and you may congratulate me if you like. She'll marry me, in spite of everything!"

"Well, then," I returned, "all I can say is that you may eliminate the one exception

which you and I agreed to make from our
estimate of the female sex at large the other
day. How is a reasonable male creature to
account for such behaviour? It is as absurd
for her to think of marrying you now as it is
for you to think of marrying her. I don't
see what you mean by it—either of you. Why,
it isn't a week since you were upon the verge
of proposing to Miss St George, and it isn't a
week since she solemnly assured me that she
had quite got over her—"

I checked myself; but not in time to prevent
him from divining the conclusion of my un-
finished sentence.

"She did, then!" he cried triumphantly. "I
was sure of it—I knew she had loved me, just
as I loved her, from the very first; only she
wouldn't admit it. Now, look here, my dear
Martyn; you mustn't be crabbed and unpleasant
about this, because it's all settled, and we know
very well what we are going in for. As Nora
says, we are neither of us people of expensive
tastes—"

"Merciful Heavens!" I ejaculated, "does she say that you are not a person of expensive tastes? If she'll say that, she'll say anything; I give her up."

"Neither of us people of expensive tastes," resumed Hurstbourne composedly, "and we shall rather enjoy wandering about Europe and living on second floors for a year or two. Oh, it wasn't the money part of the business that I was afraid of! But, thank God! Nora knows all about my poor father, and it hasn't made a bit of difference in her. She says she doesn't think it would have made very much difference if I had been a forger myself."

"Don't I tell you that she would say anything! I suppose it didn't strike either you or her that there would be a certain propriety in asking for my consent."

"Oh, yes, it did; we shall be inconsolable if you don't give your consent. Only, that won't prevent us from marrying without it, you know. Think it over, old chap, and don't look so glum about it. I must run down and see my mother now. Of course she is to live with us while we are abroad; Nora made a point of that."

What further proof could I require that my unhappy sister had ceased to be a reponsible being?

CHAPTER XI.

VENIT HESPERUS : ITE CAPELLÆ !

I DOUBT whether poor Lady Charles was altogether enchanted by the news of her son's engagement, coupled though it was with the announcement of a plan for her future well-being at which she had the good sense to laugh. Truth to tell, the match was neither a brilliant nor an opportune one, and some credit was due to her for giving her consent to it almost without hesitation. To be sure, she would have consented to Hurstbourne's marriage with a negress if his heart had really been set upon so grievous an alliance, for she was one of those women whom Heaven has blessed with a sincere belief that the persons whom they love can do no wrong. *Terque, quaterque beatae !* we admire or deride them, as our individual temperaments may dictate,

199

but, whatever verdict we may see fit to pass upon them, we can hardly deny them the tribute of our envy.

As for my consent, I have already intimated that that was not held worthy of a second thought by those who might have remembered that I was, after all, the head of my insignificant family and the legitimate protector of my only sister. Nora, when she came to make her necessary confession to me, was pleased to carry things off with a very high hand. She told me in so many words that she didn't care an atom whether her conduct struck me as inconsistent or not. She said her life was her own and she had a right to do as she pleased with it. Furthermore, she took the liberty to insinuate that, if I didn't consider the Duke of Hurstbourne one of the noblest and most exemplary of contemporary magnates, I must have singularly misused the pportunities which had been granted to me of studying his character.

"My dear girl," I ventured to remonstrate; "you surely can't have forgotten that-

your swan was a goose only the other day.
Who deplored his unfortunate weakness? Who
urged her brother to act as a benevolent men-
tor to him? Who was never weary of impress-
ing upon me that he would always be sure
to do what those about him did?"

"I never called him a goose," she affirmed
unblushingly. "I did think that he was liable
to be deceived, and it is just because he is
so much better and simpler than commonplace
folks like you and me that he was in danger
of being taken in. Only he hasn't been, you
see"

"I'm not so sure about that," I returned. "If
he hasn't been taken in by you, you may depend upon it that most people will say he has."

"Let them," answered Nora, with her chin
in the air; "we can very well afford to despise
them and their ill - natured tittle - tattle. So
long as *he* is satisfied and Lady Charles is
satisfied, they may say anything they like for
me. Of course I want you to be satisfied too,
Phil," she added, by way of a complimentary
after-thought.

My satisfaction was not, I own, wholly un-
alloyed. It is a proud thing, no doubt, to be
the brother-in-law of a duke; yet, notwithstanding the fine independence of one's temperament
and principles, there are certain accusations for
which one would rather not afford an excuse,
and I could hear in advance the pleasant
speeches which would be made when it should
transpire that this duke was about to espouse
the sister of his factotum. Moreover, I didn't
for a moment believe that they would manage
to keep out of debt. It was all very fine to
talk about living on second floors; but to live
on the second floor of the Hôtel Bristol in
Paris, for example—and that was just the sort
of thing that Hurstbourne would do—a man
ought to have an income of at least £5000,
and what I wanted him to do was to live for
three or four years upon considerably less than
half that sum. However, I was very soon
made aware that any remonstrance of mine
would be regarded as pure impertinences, so I
hardened my heart and endeavoured to persuade myself that my skin was thick enough,

or ought to be thick enough, to withstand the pin-pricks. Lady Charles, for her part, was so kind as to assure me that she did not hold me in the least to blame for what had occurred, She added that she had a strong personal affection for her future daughter-in-law and that, although Arthur might have done better, he might easily have done worse.

"When you come to think of it, his father married *me*," she remarked, with a quaint touch of humility which I did not feel entitled to resent.

As regards those pin-pricks, I may say that I received a sufficient number of them in due course; though Hurstbourne, I believe, escaped such annoyances. Perhaps his friends were content to pity him; perhaps they may have had a not altogether mistaken impression that he was an awkward customer to quarrel with. What I can answer for is that Lady Deverell didn't quarrel with him; on the contrary, she sent Nora a very kind letter of congratulation and a pair of silver-backed brushes as a wedding present. Paul

Gascoigne did not rise to quite that height of magnanimity; but when I ran against him, one day, in the street, he stopped me to explain at some length that he did not propose to take any further steps in the matter that I knew of.

"I think," he observed, "I made it clear to you and to my cousin—at all events, I intended to do so—that action on my side was simply and solely contingent upon action on his; I have no desire to punish him, now that he has recognised in so practical a manner the propriety of yielding to my demands. What need there was for the outrageous attack which he chose to make upon me I am at a loss to understand; the part which you took in the affair, Mr Martyn, is perhaps more readily comprehensible."

That was one of the above-mentioned pinpricks to which I had to submit; I can't say that it inflicted very severe suffering upon me. The same weekly journal which informed its readers of a rumour that "the youngest of our unmarried Dukes, having failed to astonish the world by a brief and far from brilliant turf career, is about to achieve the notoriety that he covets by contracting a matrimonial alliance with a young woman of obscure origin," contained a more respectful paragraph to the effect that a marriage had been arranged and would shortly take place between Mr Paul Gascoigne M.P., the nephew and residuary legatee of the late Duke of Hurstbourne, and Miss Leila St George, whose claim to take rank amongst the prominent beauties of the expiring season had been universally admitted.

When this very impertinent and mendacious newspaper fell into the hands of Lady Charles, her indignation was extreme. She was for having the editor beaten within an inch of his life forthwith, and expressed great astonishment that Hurstbourne and I, who were so ready to inflict personal chastisement upon people whom we didn't like, should hesitate to beard such a scurrilous rascal in his editorial den.

"'Obscure origin,' indeed! And you stand

smiling there, Mr Martyn, as if you thought it rather a good joke that your sister should be publicly insulted!"

"But suppose the insulting statement should be true?" I suggested. "Suppose our great-grandfather should have been, as I strongly suspect that he was, an altogether obscure individual? No, my dear Lady Charles, we had better not dispute our obscurity; but we may give this imaginative writer the lie by showing that we really don't covet notoriety. If Hurstbourne will take my advice, he will get his wedding over very quickly and quietly and leave England immediately afterwards."

Upon that point Nora was quite of one mind with me; she wished, if that could be managed, that her wedding should take place with the utmost secrecy at Dover or Folkestone an hour or so before the departure of one of the Channel boats. But Hurstbourne demurred a little. He said he didn't see why they should be married in a hole and corner way, as if they were ashamed of themselves; he hoped his wife would never have reason

to be ashamed of him, and most certainly he
should never feel otherwise than proud of
her; he was in favour of the parish church
of St George's, Hanover Square, with a
bishop, a full choir, plenty of flowers and
the requisite supply of red cloth. Eventually
a compromise was arrived at which combined
seemliness with a total absence of ostentation.
Nora was married from our uncle's house at
a small church at Kensington, and only a
few near relatives of the contracting parties
(the contracting parties hadn't a large number
of near relatives) were invited to the ceremony, which was solemnised at a time of
the year when the fashionable world had
deserted London.

When it was all over, and the bride and bride-
groom had set out for Paris, on their way to the
Tyrol, Lady Charles betook herself to Brighton,
which had always been a favourite resort of the
hers, while I journeyed north to Hurstbourne
Castle all by myself. The place was to be let
for a term of years, but there were still a good
many arrangements to be made before it could

be prepared for the reception of a tenant, and
as I had nothing else to do, I had undertaken
to supervise these. To keep Hurstbourne quiet,
I had also promised that I would continue for
the present to draw my usual salary, a promise
which was the more easily made because I had
taken care to draw no salary at all for a long
time past. It was impossible to make him
understand that he couldn't give away what
he hadn't got.

I can't say that the remainder of that summer
was a very agreeable or a very satisfactory
period to me. Nothing so scandalous had ever
before been contemplated as the letting of
Hurstbourne Castle to some wealthy commercial personage, and, naturally enough, the
tenants as well as the household servants were
rather short in their manner when I attempted
to approach them upon the old friendly terms.
I daresay they might have forgiven me if the
Duke had not married my sister; but that his
marriage had something to do with his mis-
fortunes was an idea which had evidently
taken firm possession of their minds, though

they refrained from giving actual utterance to it. Then, early in the autumn, came the news of Mr Gascoigne's nuptials and of his imminent home-coming with his bride, which may have led them to draw distressing and invidious comparisons.

"I did hear, sir," Mr Higgins had the doubtful taste to remark to me, "that his Grace was rather sweet upon the young lady at one time. Well, I wish it was his Grace that was bringing of her home now—that I do!"

In default of his Grace, Mrs Gascoigne was brought home by a husband who, unlike Hurstbourne, was enabled to lavish upon her all the luxuries that money could buy, and, from what I heard, she had no notion of allowing his money to lie idle in his pocket. Having to ride over to the neighbourhood of Lavenham upon a matter of business one day, I encountered her, driving a pair of well-matched cobs, and she pulled up to inquire what news I had of the exiles.

"I am so sorry for the poor Duke," she was kind enough to say; "I know how he must hate foreign life, and how frightfully bored he must be. Still, under the circumstances, it is just as well, perhaps, that he should remain out of sight until people have had time to forget what a fool he has made— oh, I beg your pardon, I quite forgot that you were his brother-in-law now. Please give him my kindest remembrances when you write, and tell him that we have some idea of becoming his tenants. Mr Gascoigne feels that the Castle ought to be occupied by one of the family; so, if he doesn't want too exorbitant a rent for the place, we may take it off his hands."

"Am I to consider this a formal offer, Mrs Gascoigne?" I inquired.

She hesitated for a moment, and then re-replied—

"Well, you can mention it when you write, anyhow. Personally, I should be only too glad to do anything that I could to help him out of his embarrassments, poor fellow!"

It is scarcely necessary for me to say that I did not transmit the above kindly message. Some weeks later it became my duty to transmit to my brother-in-law a message of an infinitely more agreeable character. Amongst the entailed estates which he had inherited was a barren tract of land, lying some twenty or thirty miles to the northward of the Castle, which, in the late Duke's time, had gradually fallen out of cultivation, owing to the poverty of the soil, and which we now retained in our hands for grazing purposes. It was of little value, as we thought, for that or any other purpose; but a few months before, a suspicion had arisen of the existence of coal beneath the surface, and, permission having been obtained to make investigations, the suspicion had by this time become converted into a certainty. I had said nothing about it to Hurstbourne because I knew that, if he were told, he would at once jump to the conclusion that boundless wealth was within his grasp and would act accordingly; but now I could no longer conceal from him the fact that he owned a property the value of which might be very great indeed.

He behaved much more coolly and sensibly

than I had expected. He gave me full powers
to make such arrangements as might seem
advisable to me, merely remarking that, although
he should like very well to be a rich man, he
was perfectly happy as a poor one. He wrote
from Venice, where he stated that Nora and
he were having a glorious time of it. If they
didn't spend the winter there, they would spend
it in "some such place," he supposed. For
his own part, he was game to go any place
that Nora might fancy.

How long this mood would have lasted, or
into what sort of a poor man Hurstbourne
would have developed if he had remained poor,
it is difficult to say. The problem can never
now be removed from the calm sphere of
hypothesis, for it appears that there is coal
enough beneath that waste land of his to keep
the fires of his descendants alight for many
generations to come.

Nora and he returned home early in the ensuing year, by which time there was no longer
any question of letting the abode of his an-
cestors. They were met, of course, by an en-

thusiastic welcome on the part of their tenautry and other dependents, which was, I hope, as much a tribute to their personal merits as to their improved circumstances. But, charitable as I am, I cannot go quite so far as to believe that Nora's unassisted merits would ever have placed her upon that pinnacle in high society which she now occupies with so much ease and elegance. We live in an age when aristocracy is almost, if not yet altogether, synonymous with wealth, and the philosophic bystanders must be content to note, with rejoicing, that every now and then wealth does, by some happy accident, fall to those who know how to use it. One of the best uses to which it can be put is to distribute it judiciously amongst the many who toil in penury, so that the few may be rich, and I must say for my sister and her husband that they do their duty very fairly well in that particular. It is needless to add that Hurstbourne has returned to the turf; but he is now so big a man that he can afford to eschew the bookmakers, and he is going in for breeding, which is a far more sportsman-like and satisfactory phase of the pursuit than purchasing animals in whom it must be difficult to feel anything beyond a pecuniary interest. The Duchess of Hurstbourne and Mrs Paul Gascoigne are not exactly friends; but they speak when they meet, and I can answer for it that one of them abstains from saying nasty things about the other behind her back.

Only a few days ago I heard a piece of news which had the privilege of amusing me. I always knew that Lady Deverell held the rector of her parish in high and deserved veneration, but I never thought that she would display it in so striking a fashion as by the removal of him and his numerous olive branches from the Rectory to Fern Hill. That, however, is actually what she means to do. I had it from her own lips, so that there can be no mistake about it.

"I can see by your face," she remarked candidly, "that you think me an old fool, but perhaps I may not be quite such a fool as I look. Although I am old, I have an iron con-

stitution. I may live for another twenty or
even thirty years; it isn't in the least unlikely;
and I don't enjoy living alone. Mr Burgess
will, at any rate, give me the company of a
man whom I admire and esteem. As for the
children—well, I have a large house, and I do
not intend to surrender the control of my
money to anybody. I needn't say that at Mr
Burgess's time of life and mine, we aren't such
idiots as to talk about marrying for love. He
assures me that he never was really enamoured
of your sister, and to tell you the truth, I
shouldn't have cared a straw if he had been.
As you know, there was a man once upon a
time for whom I did care, and who was not
worth caring for. I have forgiven him now.
One forgives, let me tell you, Mr Martyn, chiefly
because one forgets, and one forgets because
one can't help it."

"It is a pity," I made so bold as to remark,
"that you couldn't manage to forgive and forget Lord Charles Gascoigne a little sooner."

"I can understand your thinking so; yet I
did no more than I felt bound to do, and I

can't see that much harm has come of it. It is true that although one forgets most things, there are one or two which can't be forgotten, and I suspect that if your young Duke lives to be twice my age, he will never succeed in forgetting altogether what his father was. So if I had a grudge against him, I daresay we may cry quits."

There is no denying that Lady Deverell is a singularly disagreeable old woman.

THE END.

A LIST OF NEW BOOKS AND ANNOUNCEMENTS OF METHUEN AND COMPANY PUBLISHERS : LONDON 18 BURY STREET W.C.

CONTENTS

OCTOBER 1892

MESSRS. METHUEN'S
AUTUMN ANNOUNCEMENTS

---◆---

GENERAL LITERATURE

udyard **Kipling.** BARRACK-ROOM BALLADS; And Other Verses. By RUDYARD KIPLING. *Extra Post 8vo, pp.* 208. *Laid paper, rough edges, buckram, gilt top.* 6s.

A special Presentation Edition, *bound in white buckram, with extra gilt ornament.* 7s. 6d.

The First Edition was sold on publication, and two further large Editions have been exhausted. The Fourth Edition is Now Ready.

ladstone. THE SPEECHES AND PUBLIC ADDRESSES OF THE RT. HON. W. E. GLADSTONE, M.P. With Notes. Edited by A. W. HUTTON, M.A. (Librarian of the Gladstone Library), and H. J. COHEN, M.A. With Portraits. *8vo. Vol. IX.* 12s. 6d.

Messrs. METHUEN beg to announce that they are about to issue, in ten volumes 8vo, an authorised collection of Mr. Gladstone's Speeches, the work being undertaken with his sanction and under his superintendence. Notes and Introductions will be added.

In view of the interest in the Home Rule Question, it is proposed to issue Vols. IX. and X., which will include the speeches of the last seven or eight years, immediately, and then to proceed with the earlier volumes. Volume X. is already published.

ollingwood. JOHN RUSKIN: His Life and Work. By W. G. COLLINGWOOD, M.A., late Scholar of University College, Oxford, Author of the 'Art Teaching of John Ruskin,' Editor of Mr. Ruskin's Poems. *2 vols. 8vo.* 32s.

Also a limited edition on hand-made paper, with the Illustrations on India paper. £3, 3s. *net.*

Also a small edition on Japanese paper. £5, 5s. *net.*

This important work is written by Mr. Collingwood, who has been for some years Mr. Ruskin's private secretary, and who has had unique advantages in obtaining materials for this book from Mr. Ruskin himself and from his friends. It will contain a large amount of new matter, and of letters which have never been published, and will be, in fact, as near as is possible at present, a full and authoritative biography of Mr. Ruskin. The book will contain numerous portraits of Mr. Ruskin, including a coloured one from a water-colour portait by himself, and also 13 sketches, never before published, by Mr. Ruskin and Mr. Arthur Severn. A bibliography will be added.

Baring Gould. THE TRAGEDY OF THE CAESARS: The Emperors of the Julian and Claudian Lines. With numerous Illustrations from Busts, Gems, Cameos, etc. By S. BARING GOULD, Author of 'Mehalah,' etc. *2 vols. Royal 8vo.* 30*s.*

This book is the only one in English which deals with the personal history of the Caesars, and Mr. Baring Gould has found a subject which, for picturesque detail and sombre interest, is not rivalled by any work of fiction. The volumes are copiously illustrated.

Baring Gould. SURVIVALS AND SUPERSTITIONS. With Illustrations. By S. BARING GOULD. *Crown 8vo.* 7*s.* 6*d.*

A book on such subjects as Foundations, Gables, Holes, Gallows, Raising the Hat, Old Ballads, etc. etc. It traces in a most interesting manner their origin and history.

Perrens. THE HISTORY OF FLORENCE FROM THE TIME OF THE MEDICIS TO THE FALL OF THE REPUBLIC. By F. T. PERRENS. Translated by HANNAH LYNCH. In three volumes. Vol. I. *8vo.* 12*s.* 6*d.*

This is a translation from the French of the best history of Florence in existence. This volume covers a period of profound interest—political and literary—and is written with great vivacity.

Henley & Whibley. A BOOK OF ENGLISH PROSE. Collected by W. E. HENLEY and CHARLES WHIBLEY. *Crown 8vo.* 6*s.*

Also small limited editions on Dutch and Japanese paper. 21*s.* and 42*s.*

A companion book to Mr. Henley's well-known *Lyra Heroica.*

"Q." GREEN BAYS : A Book of Verses. By "Q.," Author of 'Dead Man's Rock' &c. *Fcap. 8vo.* 3*s.* 6*d.*

Also a limited edition on large Dutch paper.

A small volume of Oxford Verses by the well-known author of 'I Saw Three Ships, etc.

Wells. OXFORD AND OXFORD LIFE. By Members of the University. Edited by J. WELLS, M.A., Fellow and Tutor of Wadham College. *Crown 8vo.* 3*s.* 6*d.*

This work will be of great interest and value to all who are in any way connected with the University. It will contain an account of life at Oxford—intellectual, social, and religious—a careful estimate of necessary expenses, a review of recent changes, a statement of the present position of the University, and chapters on Women's Education, aids to study, and University Extension.

Driver. SERMONS ON SUBJECTS CONNECTED WITH THE OLD TESTAMENT. By S. R. DRIVER, D.D., Canon of Christ Church, Regius Professor of Hebrew in the University of Oxford. *Crown 8vo.* 6*s.*

An important volume of sermons on Old Testament Criticism preached before the University by the author of 'An Introduction to the Literature of the Old Testament.'

Prior. CAMBRIDGE SERMONS. Edited by C. H. PRIOR, M.A., Fellow and Tutor of Pembroke College. *Crown 8vo.* 6s.

A volume of sermons preached before the University of Cambridge by various preachers, including the Archbishop of Canterbury and Bishop Westcott.

Kaufmann. CHARLES KINGSLEY. By M. KAUFMANN, M.A. *Crown 8vo.* 5s.

A biography of Kingsley, especially dealing with his achievements in social reform.

Lock. THE LIFE OF JOHN KEBLE. By WALTER LOCK, M.A., Fellow of Magdalen College, Oxford. With Portrait. *Crown 8vo.* 5s.

Hutton. CARDINAL MANNING: A Biography. By A. W. HUTTON, M.A. With Portrait. *New and Cheaper Edition. Crown 8vo.* 2s. 6d.

Sells. THE MECHANICS OF DAILY LIFE. By V. P. SELLS, M.A. Illustrated. *Crown 8vo.* 2s. 6d.

Kimmins. THE CHEMISTRY OF LIFE AND HEALTH. By C. W. KIMMINS, Downing College, Cambridge. Illustrated. *Crown 8vo.* 2s. 6d.

Potter. AGRICULTURAL BOTANY. By M. C. POTTER, Lecturer at Newcastle College of Science. Illustrated. *Crown 8vo.* 2s. 6d.

The above are new volumes of the "University Extension Series."

Cox. LAND NATIONALISATION. By HAROLD COX, M.A. *Crown 8vo.* 2s. 6d.

Hadfield & Gibbins. A SHORTER WORKING DAY. By R. A. HADFIELD and H. de B. GIBBINS, M.A. *Crown 8vo.* 2s. 6d.

The above are new volumes of "Social Questions of To-day" Series.

FICTION.

Norris. HIS GRACE. By W. E. NORRIS, Author of 'Mdle. de Mersac,' 'Marcia,' etc. *Crown 8vo.* 2 vols. 21s.

Pryce. TIME AND THE WOMAN. By RICHARD PRYCE, Author of 'Miss Maxwell's Affections,' 'The Quiet Mrs. Fleming,' etc. *Crown 8vo.* 2 vols. 21s.

Parker. PIERRE AND HIS PEOPLE. By GILBERT PARKER. *Crown 8vo. Buckram.* 6s.

Marriott Watson. DIOGENES OF LONDON and other Sketches. By H. B. MARRIOTT WATSON, Author of 'The Web of the Spider.' *Crown 8vo. Buckram. 6s.*

Baring Gould. IN THE ROAR OF THE SEA. By S. BARING GOULD, Author of 'Mehalah,' 'Urith,' etc. Cheaper edition. *Crown 8vo. 6s.*

Clark Russell. MY DANISH SWEETHEART. By W. CLARK RUSSELL, Author of 'The Wreck of the Grosvenor,' 'A Marriage at Sea,' etc. With 6 Illustrations by W. H. OVEREND. *Crown 8vo. 6s.*

Mabel Robinson. HOVENDEN, V. C. By F. MABEL ROBINSON, Author of 'Disenchantment,' etc. Cheaper Edition. *Crown 8vo. 3s. 6d.*

Meade. OUT OF THE FASHION. By L. T. MEADE, Author of 'A Girl of the People,' etc. With 6 Illustrations by W. PAGET. *Crown 8vo. 6s.*

Cuthell. ONLY A GUARDROOM DOG. By Mrs. CUTHELL. With 16 Illustrations by W. PARKINSON. *Square Crown 8vo. 6s.*

Collingwood. THE DOCTOR OF THE JULIET. By HARRY COLLINGWOOD, Author of 'The Pirate Island,' etc. Illustrated by GORDON BROWNE. *Crown 8vo. 6s.*

Bliss. A MODERN ROMANCE. By LAURENCE BLISS. *Crown 8vo. Buckram. 3s. 6d. Paper. 2s. 6d.*

CHEAPER EDITIONS.

Baring Gould. OLD COUNTRY LIFE. By S. BARING GOULD, Author of 'Mehalah,' etc. With 67 Illustrations. *Crown 8vo. 6s.*

Clark. THE COLLEGES OF OXFORD. Edited by A. CLARK, M.A., Fellow and Tutor of Lincoln College. *8vo. 12s. 6d.*

Russell. THE LIFE OF ADMIRAL LORD COLLING-WOOD. By W. CLARK RUSSELL, Author of 'The Wreck of the Grosvenor.' With Illustrations by F. BRANGWYN. *8vo. 10s. 6d.*

Author of 'Mdle. Mori.' THE SECRET OF MADAME DE Monluc. By the Author of 'The Atelier du Lys,' 'Mdle. Mori.' *Crown 8vo. 3s. 6d.*

'An exquisite literary cameo.'—*World.*

𝔑𝔢𝔴 𝔞𝔫𝔡 𝔯𝔢𝔠𝔢𝔫𝔱 𝔅𝔬𝔬𝔨𝔰.

Poetry

Rudyard Kipling. BARRACK-ROOM BALLADS; And Other Verses. By RUDYARD KIPLING. *Fourth Edition. Crown 8vo. 6s.*

'Mr. Kipling's verse is strong, vivid, full of character. . . . Unmistakable genius rings in every line.'—*Times.*

'The disreputable lingo of Cockayne is henceforth justified before the world ; for a man of genius has taken it in hand, and has shown, beyond all cavilling, that in its way it also is a medium for literature. You are grateful, and you say to yourself, half in envy and half in admiration : " Here is a *book* ; here, or one is a Dutchman, is one of the books of the year." '—*National Observer.*

' " Barrack-Room Ballads " contains some of the best work that Mr. Kipling has ever done, which is saying a good deal. " Fuzzy-Wuzzy," " Gunga Din," and " Tommy," are, in our opinion, altogether superior to anything of the kind that English literature has hitherto produced.'—*Athenæum.*

'These ballads are as wonderful in their descriptive power as they are vigorous in their dramatic force. There are few ballads in the English language more stirring than "The Ballad of East and West," worthy to stand by the Border ballads of Scott.'—*Spectator.*

'The ballads teem with imagination, they palpitate with emotion. We read them with laughter and tears ; the metres throb in our pulses, the cunningly ordered words tingle with life ; and if this be not poetry, what is?'—*Pall Mall Gazette.*

bsen. BRAND. A Drama by HENRIK IBSEN. Translated by WILLIAM WILSON. *Crown 8vo. 5s.*

'The greatest world-poem of the nineteenth century next to "Faust." "Brand" will have an astonishing interest for Englishmen. It is in the same set with "Agamemnon," with "Lear," with the literature that we now instinctively regard as high and holy.'—*Daily Chronicle.*

enley. LYRA HEROICA : An Anthology selected from the best English Verse of the 16th, 17th, 18th, and 19th Centuries. By WILLIAM ERNEST HENLEY, Author of 'A Book of Verse,' 'Views and Reviews,' etc. *Crown 8vo. Stamped gilt buckram, gilt top, edges uncut. 6s.*

'Mr. Henley has brought to the task of selection an instinct alike for poetry and for chivalry which seems to us quite wonderfully, and even unerringly, right.'—*Guardian.*

omson. A SUMMER NIGHT, AND OTHER POEMS. By GRAHAM R. TOMSON. With Frontispiece by A. TOMSON. *Fcap. 8vo. 3s. 6d.*

Also an edition on handmade paper, limited to 50 copies. *Large crown 8vo. 10s. 6d. net.*

'Mrs. Tomson holds perhaps the very highest rank among poetesses of English birth. This selection will help her reputation.'—*Black and White.*

angbridge. A CRACKED FIDDLE. Being Selections from the Poems of FREDERIC LANGBRIDGE. With Portrait. *Crown 8vo.* 5*s.*

angbridge. BALLADS OF THE BRAVE: Poems of Chivalry, Enterprise, Courage, and Constancy, from the Earliest Times to the Present Day. Edited, with Notes, by Rev. F. LANGBRIDGE. *Crown 8vo.*

Presentation Edition, 3*s.* 6*d.* School Edition, 2*s.* 6*d.*

'A very happy conception happily carried out. These "Ballads of the Brave" are intended to suit the real tastes of boys, and will suit the taste of the great majority. —*Spectator.* 'The book is full of splendid things.'—*World.*

History and Biography

ladstone. THE SPEECHES AND PUBLIC ADDRESSES OF THE RT. HON. W. E. GLADSTONE, M.P. With Notes and Introductions. Edited by A. W. HUTTON, M.A. (Librarian of the Gladstone Library), and H. J. COHEN, M.A. With Portraits. *8vo.* *Vol. X.* 12*s.* 6*d.*

ussell. THE LIFE OF ADMIRAL LORD COLLING-WOOD. By W. CLARK RUSSELL, Author of 'The Wreck of the Grosvenor.' With Illustrations by F. BRANGWYN. *8vo.* 10*s.* 6*d.*

'A really good book.'—*Saturday Review.*
'A most excellent and wholesome book, which we should like to see in the hands of every boy in the country.'—*St. James's Gazette.*

lark. THE COLLEGES OF OXFORD: Their History and their Traditions. By Members of the University. Edited by A. CLARK, M.A., Fellow and Tutor of Lincoln College. *8vo.* 12*s.* 6*d.*

'Whether the reader approaches the book as a patriotic member of a college, as an antiquary, or as a student of the organic growth of college foundation, it will amply reward his attention.'—*Times.*
'A delightful book, learned and lively.'—*Academy.*
'A work which will certainly be appealed to for many years as the standard book on the Colleges of Oxford.'—*Athenæum.*

ulton. RIXAE OXONIENSES: An Account of the Battles of the Nations, The Struggle between Town and Gown, etc. By S. F. HULTON, M.A. *Crown 8vo.* 5*s.*

ames. CURIOSITIES OF CHRISTIAN HISTORY PRIOR TO THE REFORMATION. By CROAKE JAMES, Author of 'Curiosities of Law and Lawyers.' *Crown 8vo.* 7*s.* 6*d.*

Clifford. THE DESCENT OF CHARLOTTE COMPTON (BARONESS FERRERS DE CHARTLEY). By her Great-Granddaughter, ISABELLA G. C. CLIFFORD. *Small 4to.* 10s. 6d. *net.*

General Literature

Bowden. THE IMITATION OF BUDDHA: Being Quotations from Buddhist Literature for each Day in the Year. Compiled by E. M. BOWDEN. With Preface by Sir EDWIN ARNOLD. *Second Edition.* 16mo. 2s. 6d.

Ditchfield. OUR ENGLISH VILLAGES: Their Story and their Antiquities. By P. H. DITCHFIELD, M.A., F.R.H.S., Rector of Barkham, Berks. *Post 8vo.* 2s. 6d. Illustrated.

'An extremely amusing and interesting little book, which should find a place in every parochial library.'—*Guardian.*

Ditchfield. OLD ENGLISH SPORTS. By P. H. DITCHFIELD, M.A. *Crown 8vo.* 2s. 6d. Illustrated.

'A charming account of old English Sports.'—*Morning Post.*

Burne. PARSON AND PEASANT: Chapters of their Natural History. By J. B. BURNE, M.A., Rector of Wasing. *Crown 8vo.* 5s.

'"Parson and Peasant" is a book not only to be interested in, but to learn something from—a book which may prove a help to many a clergyman, and broaden the hearts and ripen the charity of laymen."'—*Derby Mercury.*

Massee. A MONOGRAPH OF THE MYXOGASTRES. By G. MASSEE. *8vo.* 18s. *net.*

Cunningham. THE PATH TOWARDS KNOWLEDGE: Essays on Questions of the Day. By W. CUNNINGHAM, D.D., Fellow of Trinity College, Cambridge, Professor of Economics at King's College, London. *Crown 8vo.* 4s. 6d.

Essays on Marriage and Population, Socialism, Money, Education, Positivism, etc.

Anderson Graham. NATURE IN BOOKS: Studies in Literary Biography. By P. ANDERSON GRAHAM. *Crown 8vo.* 6s.

The chapters are entitled: I. 'The Magic of the Fields' (Jefferies). II. 'Art and Nature' (Tennyson). III. 'The Doctrine of Idleness' (Thoreau). IV. 'The Romance of Life' (Scott). V. 'The Poetry of Toil' (Burns). VI. 'The Divinity of Nature' (Wordsworth).

Works by **S. Baring Gould.**

Author of ' Mehalah,' etc.

OLD COUNTRY LIFE. With Sixty-seven Illustrations by W. PARKINSON, F. D. BEDFORD, and F. MASEY. *Large Crown 8vo, cloth super extra, top edge gilt,* 10s. 6d. *Fourth and Cheaper Edition.* 6s. [*Ready.*

'"Old Country Life," as healthy wholesome reading, full of breezy life and move-ment, full of quaint stories vigorously told, will not be excelled by any book to be published throughout the year. Sound, hearty, and English to the core.'— *World.*

HISTORIC ODDITIES AND STRANGE EVENTS. *Third Edition, Crown 8vo.* 6s.

'A collection of exciting and entertaining chapters. The whole volume is delightful reading.'—*Times.*

FREAKS OF FANATICISM. (First published as Historic Oddities, Second Series.) *Third Edition. Crown 8vo.* 6s.

'Mr. Baring Gould has a keen eye for colour and effect, and the subjects he has chosen give ample scope to his descriptive and analytic faculties. A perfectly fascinating book.—*Scottish Leader.*

SONGS OF THE WEST: Traditional Ballads and Songs of the West of England, with their Traditional Melodies. Collected by S. BARING GOULD, M.A., and H. FLEETWOOD SHEPPARD, M.A. Arranged for Voice and Piano. In 4 Parts (containing 25 Songs each), *Parts I., II., III.,* 3s. *each. Part IV.,* 5s. *In one Vol., roan,* 15s.

'A rich and varied collection of humour, pathos, grace, and poetic fancy.'—*Saturday Review.*

YORKSHIRE ODDITIES AND STRANGE EVENTS. *Fourth Edition. Crown 8vo.* 6s.

SURVIVALS AND SUPERSTITIONS. *Crown 8vo.* Illustrated. [*In the press.*

JACQUETTA, and other Stories. *Crown 8vo.* 3s. 6d. *Boards,* 2s.

ARMINELL: A Social Romance. *New Edition. Crown 8vo.* 3s. 6d. *Boards,* 2s.

'To say that a book is by the author of "Mehalah" is to imply that it contains a story cast on strong lines, containing dramatic possibilities, vivid and sympathetic descriptions of Nature, and a wealth of ingenious imagery. All these expecta-tions are justified by "Arminell."'—*Speaker.*

URITH: A Story of Dartmoor. *Third Edition. Crown 8vo.* 3s. 6

'The author is at his best.'—*Times.*
'He has nearly reached the high water-mark of "Mehalah."'—*National Observer.*

MARGERY OF QUETHER, and other Stories. *Crown 8vo* 3s. 6d.

IN THE ROAR OF THE SEA: A Tale of the Cornish Coast *New Edition.* 6s.

Fiction

Author of 'Indian Idylls.' IN TENT AND BUNGALOW Stories of Indian Sport and Society. By the Author of 'India Idylls.' *Crown 8vo.* 3s. 6d.

Fenn. A DOUBLE KNOT. By G. MANVILLE FENN, Autho of 'The Vicar's People,' etc. *Crown 8vo.* 3s. 6d.

Pryce. THE QUIET MRS. FLEMING. By RICHARD PRYCE Author of 'Miss Maxwell's Affections,' etc. *Crown 8vo.* 3s. 6d *Picture Boards,* 2s.

Gray. ELSA. A Novel. By E. M'QUEEN GRAY. *Crown 8vo.* 6s

'A charming novel. The characters are not only powerful sketches, but minutel and carefully finished portraits.'—*Guardian.*

Gray. MY STEWARDSHIP. By E. M'QUEEN GRAY *Crown 8vo.* 3s. 6d.

Cobban. A REVEREND GENTLEMAN. By J. MACLARE COBBAN, Author of 'Master of his Fate,' etc. *Crown 8vo.* 4s. 6d.

'The best work Mr. Cobban has yet achieved. The Rev. W. Merrydew is a brillian creation.'—*National Observer.*
'One of the subtlest studies of character outside Meredith.'—*Star.*

Lyall. DERRICK VAUGHAN, NOVELIST. By EDN LYALL, Author of 'Donovan.' *Crown 8vo.* 31st *Thousand* 3s. 6d. ; *paper,* 1s.

Linton. THE TRUE HISTORY OF JOSHUA DAVIDSON Christian and Communist. By E. LYNN LINTON. Eleventh an Cheaper Edition. *Post 8vo.* 1s.

Grey. THE STORY OF CHRIS. By ROWLAND GREY Author of 'Lindenblumen,' etc. *Crown 8vo.* 5s.

Dicker. A CAVALIER'S LADYE. By CONSTANCE DICKER *With Illustrations. Crown 8vo.* 3s. 6d.

Dickinson. A VICAR'S WIFE. By Evelyn Dickinson. *Crown 8vo.* 6s.

Prowse. THE POISON OF ASPS. By R. Orton Prowse. *Crown 8vo.* 6s.

Taylor. THE KING'S FAVOURITE. By Una Taylor. *Crown 8vo.* 6s.

Novel Series

3/6

Messrs. Methuen will issue from time to time a Series of copyright Novels, by well-known Authors, handsomely bound, at the above popular price of three shillings and sixpence. The first volumes (ready) are :—

1. THE PLAN OF CAMPAIGN. By F. Mabel Robinson.

2. JACQUETTA. By S. Baring Gould, Author of ' Mehalah, etc.

3. MY LAND OF BEULAH. By Mrs. Leith Adams (Mrs. De Courcy Laffan).

4. ELI'S CHILDREN. By G. Manville Fenn.

5. ARMINELL : A Social Romance. By S. Baring Gould, Author of ' Mehalah,' etc.

6. DERRICK VAUGHAN, NOVELIST. With Portrait of Author. By Edna Lyall, Author of ' Donovan,' etc.

7. DISENCHANTMENT. By F. Mabel Robinson.

8. DISARMED. By M. Betham Edwards.

9. JACK'S FATHER. By W. E. Norris.

10. MARGERY OF QUETHER. By S. Baring Gould.

11. A LOST ILLUSION. By Leslie Keith.

12. A MARRIAGE AT SEA. By W. Clark Russell.

13. MR. BUTLER'S WARD. By F. Mabel Robinson.

14. URITH. By S. Baring Gould.

15. HOVENDEN, V.C. By F. Mabel Robinson.

Other Volumes will be announced in due course.

2/

ARMINELL.   By the Author of 'Mehalah.'

ELI'S CHILDREN.   By G. MANVILLE FENN.

DISENCHANTMENT.   By F. MABEL ROBINSON.

THE PLAN OF CAMPAIGN.   By F. MABEL ROBINSON.

JACQUETTA.   By the Author of 'Mehalah.'

Picture Boards.

A DOUBLE KNOT.   By G. MANVILLE FENN.

THE QUIET MRS. FLEMING.   By RICHARD PRYCE.

JACK'S FATHER.   By W. E. NORRIS.

A LOST ILLUSION.   By LESLIE KEITH.

Books for Boys and Girls

Walford.   A PINCH OF EXPERIENCE.   By L. B. WA
FORD, Author of 'Mr. Smith.'   With Illustrations by GORDO
BROWNE.   *Crown 8vo.   6s.*

'The clever authoress steers clear of namby-pamby, and invests her moral with
fresh and striking dress.   There is terseness and vivacity of style, and the illustr
tions are admirable.'—*Anti-Jacobin.*

Molesworth.   THE RED GRANGE.   By Mrs. MOLESWORT
Author of 'Carrots.'   With Illustrations by GORDON BROWN
Crown 8vo.   6s.

'A volume in which girls will delight, and beautifully illustrated.'—*Pall Ma
Gazette.*

Clark Russell.   MASTER ROCKAFELLAR'S VOYAGE.   B
W. CLARK RUSSELL, Author of 'The Wreck of the Grosvenor,' et
Illustrated by GORDON BROWNE.   *Crown 8vo.   3s. 6d.*

'Mr. Clark Russell's story of "Master Rockafellar's Voyage" will be among t
favourites of the Christmas books.   There is a rattle and "go" all through it, ar
its illustrations are charming in themselves, and very much above the average
the way in which they are produced.—*Guardian.*

Author of 'Mdle. Mori.'   THE SECRET OF MADAME D
Monluc.   By the Author of 'The Atelier du Lys,' 'Mdle. Mori
Crown 8vo.   3s. 6d.

'An exquisite literary cameo.'—*World.*

Manville Fenn. SYD BELTON : Or, The Boy who would not go to Sea. By G. MANVILLE FENN, Author of 'In the King's Name,' etc. Illustrated by GORDON BROWNE. *Crown 8vo.* 3s. 6d.

'Who among the young story-reading public will not rejoice at the sight of the old combination, so often proved admirable—a story by Manville Fenn, illustrated by Gordon Browne ! The story, too, is one of the good old sort, full of life and vigour, breeziness and fun. —*Journal of Education.*

Parr. DUMPS. By Mrs. PARR, Author of 'Adam and Eve,' 'Dorothy Fox,' etc. Illustrated by W. PARKINSON. *Crown 8vo.* 3s. 6d.

'One of the prettiest stories which even this clever writer has given the world for a long time.'—*World.*

Meade. A GIRL OF THE PEOPLE. By L. T. MEADE, Author of 'Scamp and I,' etc. Illustrated by R. BARNES. *Crown 8vo.* 3s. 6d.

'An excellent story. Vivid portraiture of character, and broad and wholesome lessons about life.'—*Spectator.*

'One of Mrs. Meade's most fascinating books.'—*Daily News.*

Meade. HEPSY GIPSY. By L. T. MEADE. Illustrated by EVERARD HOPKINS. *Crown 8vo,* 2s. 6d.

'Mrs. Meade has not often done better work than this.'—*Spectator.*

Meade. THE HONOURABLE MISS : A Tale of a Country Town. By L. T. MEADE, Author of 'Scamp and I,' 'A Girl of the People,' etc. With Illustrations by EVERARD HOPKINS. *Crown 8vo,* 3s. 6d.

Adams. MY LAND OF BEULAH. By MRS. LEITH ADAMS. With a Frontispiece by GORDON BROWNE. *Crown 8vo,* 3s. 6d.

English Leaders of Religion

Edited by A. M. M. STEDMAN, M.A. *With Portrait, crown 8vo,* 2s. 6d.

A series of short biographies, free from party bias, of the most prominent leaders of religious life and thought in this and the last century.

2/6

The following are already arranged—

CARDINAL NEWMAN. By R. H. HUTTON. [*Ready.*

'Few who read this book will fail to be struck by the wonderful insight it displays into the nature of the Cardinal's genius and the spirit of his life.'—WILFRID WARD, in the *Tablet.*

'Full of knowledge, excellent in method, and intelligent in criticism. We regard it as wholly admirable.'—*Academy.*

JOHN WESLEY. By J. H. OVERTON, M.A. [*Read*

'It is well done: the story is clearly told, proportion is duly observed, and there no lack either of discrimination or of sympathy.'—*Manchester Guardian.*

BISHOP WILBERFORCE. By G. W. DANIEL, M.A. [*Read*

CHARLES SIMEON. By H. C. G. MOULE, M.A. [*Read*

JOHN KEBLE. By W. LOCK, M.A. [*No*

F. D. MAURICE. By COLONEL F. MAURICE, R.E.

THOMAS CHALMERS. By Mrs. OLIPHANT.

CARDINAL MANNING. By A. W. HUTTON, M.A. [*Read*

Other volumes will be announced in due course.

University Extension Series

A series of books on historical, literary, and scientific subjects, suitabl for extension students and home reading circles. Each volume will t complete in itself, and the subjects will be treated by competent write in a broad and philosophic spirit.

Edited by J. E. SYMES, M.A.,
Principal of University College, Nottingham.

Crown 8vo. 2s. 6d.

2/

The following volumes are ready :—

THE INDUSTRIAL HISTORY OF ENGLAND. By H. D
B. GIBBINS, M.A., late Scholar of Wadham College, Oxon., Cobde
Prizeman. *Second Edition.* With Maps and Plans. [*Read*

'A compact and clear story of our industrial development. A study of this conci but luminous book cannot fail to give the reader a clear insight into the princip phenomena of our industrial history. The editor and publishers are to be congr tulated on this first volume of their venture, and we shall look with expecta interest for the succeeding volumes of the series.'—*University Extension Journa*

A HISTORY OF ENGLISH POLITICAL ECONOMY. B
L. L. PRICE, M.A., Fellow of Oriel College, Oxon.

PROBLEMS OF POVERTY: An Inquiry into the Industri
Conditions of the Poor. By J. A. HOBSON, M.A.

VICTORIAN POETS. By A. SHARP.

THE FRENCH REVOLUTION. By J. E. SYMES, M.A.

PSYCHOLOGY. By F. S. GRANGER, M.A., Lecturer in Philosophy at University College, Nottingham.

THE EVOLUTION OF PLANT LIFE : Lower Forms. By G. MASSEE, Kew Gardens. With Illustrations.

AIR AND WATER. Professor V. B. LEWES, M.A. Illustrated.

THE CHEMISTRY OF LIFE AND HEALTH. By C. W. KIMMINS, M.A. Camb. Illustrated.

THE MECHANICS OF DAILY LIFE. By V. P. SELLS, M.A. Illustrated.

ENGLISH SOCIAL REFORMERS. H. DE B. GIBBINS, M.A.

ENGLISH TRADE AND FINANCE IN THE SEVENTEENTH CENTURY. By W. A. S. HEWINS, B.A.

The following volumes are in preparation :—

NAPOLEON. By E. L. S. HORSBURGH, M.A. Camb., U. E. Lecturer in History.

ENGLISH POLITICAL HISTORY. By T. J. LAWRENCE, M.A., late Fellow and Tutor of Downing College, Cambridge, U. E. Lecturer in History.

AN INTRODUCTION TO PHILOSOPHY. By J. SOLOMON, M.A. Oxon., late Lecturer in Philosophy at University College, Nottingham.

THE EARTH : An Introduction to Physiography. By E. W. SMALL, M.A.

Social Questions of To-day

Edited by H. DE B. GIBBINS, M.A.

Crown 8vo, 2s. 6d.

2/6

A series of volumes upon those topics of social, economic, and industrial interest that are at the present moment foremost in the public mind. Each volume of the series will be written by an author who is an acknowledged authority upon the subject with which he deals.

The following Volumes of the Series are ready :—

TRADE UNIONISM—NEW AND OLD. By G. HOWELL, M.P., Author of ' The Conflicts of Capital and Labour.

THE CO-OPERATIVE MOVEMENT TO-DAY.   By G. J
HOLYOAKE, Author of ' The History of Co-operation.'

MUTUAL THRIFT.   By Rev. J. FROME WILKINSON, M.A
Author of ' The Friendly Society Movement.'

PROBLEMS OF POVERTY : An Inquiry into the Industria
Conditions of the Poor.   By J. A. HOBSON, M.A.

THE COMMERCE OF NATIONS.   By C. F. BASTABLE
M.A., Professor of Economics at Trinity College, Dublin.

THE ALIEN INVASION. By W. H. WILKINS, B.A., Secretar
to the Society for Preventing the Immigration of Destitute Aliens.

THE RURAL EXODUS.   By P. ANDERSON GRAHAM.

LAND NATIONALIZATION.   By HAROLD COX, B.A.

A SHORTER WORKING DAY.   By H. DE B. GIBBIN
(Editor), and R. A. HADFIELD, of the Hecla Works, Sheffield.

The following Volumes are in preparation :—

ENGLISH SOCIALISM OF TO-DAY.   By HUBERT BLAND
one of the Authors of ' Fabian Essays.'

POVERTY AND PAUPERISM. ·By Rev. L. R. PHELPS, M.A.
Fellow of Oriel College, Oxford.

ENGLISH LAND AND ENGLISH MEN.   By Rev. C. W
STUBBS, M.A., Author of ' The Labourers and the Land.'

CHRISTIAN SOCIALISM IN ENGLAND.   B, Rev. J
CARTER, M.A., of Pusey House, Oxford.

THE EDUCATION OF THE PEOPLE.   By J. R. DIGGLE
M.A., Chairman of the London School Board.

WOMEN'S WORK.   By LADY DILKE, MISS BEILLEY, an
MISS ABRAHAM.

RAILWAY PROBLEMS PRESENT AND FUTURE.   B
R. W. BARNETT, M.A., Editor of the ' Railway Times.'

Printed by T. and A. CONSTABLE, Printers to Her Majesty,
at the Edinburgh University Press.

Lightning Source UK Ltd.
Milton Keynes UK
UKHW021648021218
333216UK00012B/1693/P